The Cubs and Other Stories

The Time of the Hero

The Green House

Captain Pantoja and the Special Service

Conversation in The Cathedral

Aunt Julia and the Scriptwriter

The War of the End of the World

The Real Life of Alejandro Mayta

The Perpetual Orgy

Who Killed Palomino Molero?

The Storyteller

In Praise of the Stepmother

In Praise
of the Stepmother

In Praise
of the Stepmother

Mario Vargas Llosa

TRANSLATED BY HELEN LANE

FARRAR STRAUS GIROUX

NEW YORK

English translation copyright © 1990 by Farrar, Straus and Giroux, Inc.
Originally published in Spanish as Elogio de la madrastra,
copyright © 1988 by Mario Vargas Llosa
All rights reserved
Published simultaneously in Canada by HarperCollinsCanadaLtd
Printed in the United States of America
Designed by Cynthia Krupat
First edition, 1990

Library of Congress Cataloging-in-Publication Data
Vargas Llosa, Mario.
[Elogio de la madrastra. English]
In praise of the stepmother / Mario Vargas Llosa ; translated by
Helen Lane.—1st ed.
Translation of: Elogio de la madrastra.
I. Title.
PQ8498.32.A65E413   1990   863—dc20   90-3018

To Luis G. Berlanga
with affection and admiration

One must wear one's vices like a royal mantle, with poise. Like an aureole that one is unaware of, that one pretends not to perceive.

It is only natures entirely given over to vice whose contours do not grow blurred in the hyaline mire of the atmosphere.

Beauty is a—marvelous—vice of form.

CÉSAR MORO
Amour à mort

In Praise
of the Stepmother

One.
Doña Lucrecia's
Birthday

The day she turned forty, Doña Lucrecia found on her pillow a missive in a childish hand, each letter carefully traced with great affection:

Happy birthday, stepmother!
I haven't any money to buy you a present, but I'll study hard and be first in my class, and that will be my present. You're the best and the fairest one of all, and I dream of you every night.
  Happy birthday again!

                                        Alfonso

It was past midnight and Don Rigoberto was in the bathroom performing his ablutions, slow-paced and complicated, before going to bed. (Next to erotic painting, bodily cleanliness was his favorite leisure-time pursuit; spiritual purity concerned him far less.) Touched by the little boy's letter, Doña Lucrecia felt an irresistible impulse to go to him, to thank him for it. Those lines were really her acceptance within the family. Would he be awake? No matter! If he wasn't, she would kiss him on the forehead, very gently, so as not to wake him.

As she descended the carpeted stairs of the darkened town house on her way to Alfonso's room, she thought to herself: I've won him over. He loves me now. And her old fears about the child began to evaporate like a light snow gnawed away by the summer sun of Lima. She had neglected to put on a dressing gown; she was naked beneath her thin black silk nightdress, and the full white curves of her body, firm still, seemed to float in the shadow illuminated here and there by glancing reflections from the street. Her long hair hung loose and she had not yet removed the teardrop pendants at her ears, the rings and the necklaces that she had worn for the party.

There was a light still on in the youngster's room—Foncho certainly read far into the night! Doña Lucrecia knocked softly and went in: "Alfonsito!" In the yellowish cone of light from the little bedside lamp, there appeared, from behind a book by Alexandre Dumas, the startled little face of a Child Jesus. Rumpled golden curls, mouth agape in surprise baring a double row of gleaming white teeth, big wide-open blue eyes trying to bring her forth from the shadow of the doorway. Doña Lucrecia did not move, observing him with tender affection. What a lovely child! A born angel, one of those court pages in the elegant erotic etchings that her husband kept under quadruple lock and key.

"Is that you, stepmother?"

"What a nice letter you wrote me, Foncho. It's the best birthday present anybody has ever given me, I swear."

The boy had leapt from under the covers and was now standing on the bed. He smiled at her, his arms opened wide. As she came toward him, smiling too, Doña Lucrecia surprised—divined?—in the eyes of her stepson a gaze that changed from happiness to bewilderment and riveted itself, in astonishment, on her bosom. Good heavens, you're practically naked, she suddenly thought. How could you have forgotten your dressing gown, you idiot. What a sight for the poor boy. Had she had more to drink than she should have?

But Alfonsito's arms were now about her: "Many happy returns, stepmother!" His voice, fresh and carefree, made the night young again. Doña Lucrecia felt the slender silhouette of frail bones against her body and was reminded of a little bird. The thought crossed her mind that if she hugged him tightly to her, the child would break like a reed. With him standing on the bed, the two of them were the same height. He had twined his thin arms around her neck and was lovingly kissing her on the cheek. Doña Lucrecia embraced him, too, and one of her hands, gliding beneath his navy-blue pajama top with red stripes, made its way up his back, her fingertips feeling the delicate gradations of his vertebrae. "I love you lots, stepmother," the little voice whispered in her ear. Doña Lucrecia felt two tiny lips linger on her earlobe, warming it with their breath, kissing it and nibbling it, playing. Alfonsito appeared to her to be laughing as he caressed her. Her breast was filled to overflowing with emotion. To think that her women friends had prophesied that this stepson would be the major obstacle for her, that because of him she would never be able to be happy with Rigoberto. Deeply moved, she kissed him back, on the cheeks, the forehead, the tousled hair, as, vaguely, as though come from afar, without her having really noticed, a different sensation suffused every last confine of her body, becoming most densely concentrated in those parts—her breasts, her belly, the backs of her thighs, her neck, shoulders, cheeks—exposed to the child's touch. "Do you really love me lots?" she asked, trying to free herself from his embrace. But Alfonsito would not let her go. Instead, as he sang out in answer: "Lots and lots, stepmother, more than . . ." he clung to her. Then his little hands grasped her by the temples and thrust her head back. Doña Lucrecia felt herself being pecked on the forehead, the eyes, the eyebrows, the cheek, the chin . . . When the thin lips brushed hers, she clenched her teeth in confusion. Did Fonchito know what he was doing? Ought she to push him brusquely away? No, of course not. How could there be the least perversity in the mad fluttering of those mischievous lips that twice, three times, wandering over the geography of her face, alighted on hers for an instant, hungrily pressing down on them.

"All right, to bed with you now," she finally said, freeing herself from the boy's embrace. She did her best to appear more self-assured than she felt. "Otherwise, you won't get up in time for school, sweetie."

Nodding his head, the boy got into bed. He eyed her, laughing, his cheeks flushed a rosy pink, an ecstatic look on his face. How could there be anything perverse about him? That pure little face, those eyes filled with joy, that little body tucking itself in between the sheets and snuggling down: weren't they the personification of innocence? You're the corrupted one, Lucrecia! She pulled the covers over him, straightened his pillow, kissed his curls, and turned out the lamp on the night table.

As she was leaving the room, she heard him trill: "I'll be first in my class and that will be my present for you, stepmother."

"Is that a promise, Fonchito?"

"Word of honor!"

In the intimate complicity of the staircase, on her way back to the master bedroom, Doña Lucrecia felt on fire from head to foot. But it's not a fever, she said to herself in a daze. Could a child's unthinking caress have put her in such a state? You're becoming depraved, woman. Could this be the first symptom of old age? Because there was no question about it: she was all aflame and her thighs were wet. How disgraceful, Lucrecia, shame on you! And all of a sudden there came back to her the memory of a licentious friend who, at a benefit tea for the Red Cross, had given rise to flushed cheeks and nervous titters at her table when she told them that taking afternoon naps naked, with a young stepson raking her back with his nails, made her as hot as a fire-cracker.

Don Rigoberto was stretched out on his back, na-ked, on top of the garnet-colored bedspread with its repeated pattern of what appeared to be scorpions. In the dark room, lighted only by the glow from the street, his long, pale white silhouette, with a thick patch of hair at his chest and pubis, remained mo-tionless as Doña Lucrecia took off her slippers and lay down at his side, not touching him. Was her husband already asleep?

"Where were you?" she heard him murmur, in the thick, drawling voice of a man speaking from out of a dream-fantasy, a voice she knew so well. "Why did you leave me, darling?"

"I went to give Fonchito a kiss. He wrote me a birthday letter you wouldn't believe. So affectionate it almost made me cry."

She sensed that Don Rigoberto scarcely heard

her. She felt his right hand stroking her thigh. It burned, like a steaming-hot compress. His fingers fumbled about amid the folds of her nightdress. "He's bound to notice that I'm soaking wet," she thought uneasily. But it was a fleeting uneasiness, for the same violent wave that had startled her so on the staircase washed over her body once more, giving her gooseflesh all over. It seemed to her that all her pores were opening, waiting anxiously.

"Did Fonchito see you in your nightdress?" her husband's voice dreamed aloud, in passionate tones. "You may have given the boy wicked thoughts. Perhaps he'll have his first erotic dream tonight."

She heard him laugh excitedly, and she laughed, too. "Whatever are you saying, you idiot?" At the same time, she pretended to slap him, letting her left hand fall on Don Rigoberto's belly. But what it touched was a human staff, rising and pulsing.

"What's this? What's this?" Doña Lucrecia exclaimed, grasping it, pulling on it, letting it go, catching hold of it again. "Look what I've found. What a surprise." Don Rigoberto had already lifted her up on top of him and was kissing her with delight, sipping her lips, separating them. For a long time, with eyes closed, as she felt the tip of her husband's tongue exploring the inside of her mouth, gliding along her gums and her palate, striving to taste all of it, know all of it, Doña Lucrecia was immersed in a happy daze, a dense, palpitating sensation that seemed to make her limbs go soft and disappear, so that she felt herself floating, sinking, whirling around and around. At the bottom of the pleasant maelstrom that she found herself, found life to be, as though appearing and disappearing in a mirror that is losing its silver backing, an intrusive little face, that of a rosy-cheeked angel, was discernible from time to time. Her husband had lifted her nightgown and was stroking her buttocks, with a methodical, circular movement, as he kissed her breasts. She heard him murmur that he loved her, whisper tenderly that for him real life had begun with her. Doña Lucrecia kissed him on the neck and nibbled his nipples till she heard him moan; after that, she very slowly licked those exalted nests that Don Rigoberto had carefully washed and perfumed for her before coming to bed: his armpits.

She heard him purr like a pampered cat, wriggling beneath her body. His hands hurriedly parted Doña Lucrecia's legs, with a kind of exasperation. They placed her astride him, seated her in the proper position, opened her. She moaned, in pain and pleasure, as, in a confused whirlwind, she glimpsed an image of Saint Sebastian riddled with arrows, crucified and impaled. She had the sensation that she was being gored in the center of her heart. She could contain herself no longer. With her eyes half closed, her hands behind her head, thrusting her breasts forward, she rode that love-colt as it rocked to and fro with her, following her rhythm, mumbling words just barely articulated, till she felt herself dying, fainting, failing.

"Who am I?" she inquired blindly. "Who is it you say I've been?"

"The wife of the King of Lydia, my love," Don Rigoberto burst out, lost in his dream.

Two.
Candaules,
King of Lydia

I am Candaules, King of Lydia, a little country sit-
uated between Ionia and Caria, in the heart of that
territory which centuries later will be called Turkey.
What I am most proud of in my kingdom is not its
mountains fissured by drought or its goatherds, who,
if need be, do battle with Phrygian and Aeolian in-
vaders and Dorians come from Asia, and rout bands
of Phoenicians, Lacedaemonians, and the Scythian
nomads who come to sack our borders, but the croup
of Lucrecia, my wife.

I say and repeat the word. Not behind, or ass, or
buttocks, or backside, but croup. For when I ride
her the sensation that comes over me is precisely
this: that of being astride a velvety, muscular mare,
high-spirited and obedient. It is a hard croup and
as broad, perhaps, as it is said to be in the legends
concerning it that circulate throughout the king-

dom, inflaming my subjects' imaginations. (These accounts all reach my ears, but rather than angering me, they flatter me.) When I order her to kneel and touch her forehead to the carpet to kiss it, so that I may examine her at will, the precious object attains its most enchanting volume. Each hemisphere is a carnal paradise; the two of them, separated by a delicate cleft of nearly imperceptible down that vanishes in the forest of intoxicating whiteness, blackness, and silkiness that crowns the firm columns of her thighs, put me in mind of an altar of that barbarous religion of the Babylonians that ours expunged. It feels firm to my touch and soft to my lips; vast to my embrace and warm on cold nights, a most comfortable cushion on which to rest my head and a fountain of pleasures at the hour of amorous assault. Penetrating her is not easy; painful, rather, at first, and even heroic, in view of the resistance that those expanses of pink flesh offer to virile attack. What are required are a stubborn will and a deepplunging, persevering rod, which shrink from nothing and from no one, as is true of mine.

When I told Gyges, the son of Dascylus, my personal guard and minister, that I was prouder of the feats performed by my rod with Lucrecia in the sumptuous, full-sailed vessel of our nuptial bed than of my valorous deeds on the battlefield or of the impartiality with which I mete out justice, he whooped with laughter at what he took to be a jest. But it was not; I truly take more pride in such ex-

Jacob Jordaens, *Candaules, King of Lydia,*
showing his wife to Prime Minister Gyges (1648),
oil on canvas, The National Museum of Stockholm

ploits. I doubt that many inhabitants of Lydia can equal me. One night—I was drunk—I summoned Atlas, the best endowed of my Ethiopian slaves, to my apartments, merely to confirm that this was so. I had Lucrecia bow down before him and ordered him to mount her. Intimidated by my presence, or because it was too great a test of his strength, he was unable to do so. Again and again I saw him approach her resolutely, push, pant, and withdraw in defeat. (Since this episode vexed Lucrecia's memory, I then had Atlas beheaded.)

For it is beyond question that I love the queen. Everything about my spouse is soft, delicate, by contrast to the opulent splendor of her croup: her hands and her feet, her waist and her mouth. She has a turned-up nose and languid eyes, mysteriously still waters troubled only by pleasure and anger. I have studied her as scholars ponder the ancient volumes of the Temple, and though I think I know her by heart, each day—each night, rather—I discover something new about her that touches me: the gentle curve of her shoulders, the mischievous little bone in her elbow, the delicacy of her instep, the roundness of her knees, and the blue transparency of the little grove of her armpits.

There are those who soon tire of their lawfully wedded wife. The routine of married life kills desire, they philosophize: what illusory hope can swell and revive the veins of a man who sleeps, for months and years, with the same woman? Yet, despite our having been wed for so long a time, Lucrecia, my lady, does not bore me. I have never grown weary of her. When I go off on tiger and elephant hunts, or to make war, the memory of her makes my heart beat faster, just as in the first days, and when I caress a slave girl or some camp follower so as to relieve the loneliness of nights in a field tent, my hands always experience keen disappointment: those are merely backsides, buttocks, rumps, asses. Only hers—O beloved!—is a croup. That is why I am faithful to her in my heart; that is why I love her. That is why I compose poems to her that I recite in her ear and when we are alone prostrate myself to kiss her feet. That is why I have filled her coffers with jewels and precious stones, and ordered for her, from every corner of the world, slippers and sandals, garments, priceless ornaments she will never get around to wearing. That is why I care for her and venerate her as the most exquisite possession in my kingdom. Without Lucrecia, life would be death to me.

The real story of what happened with Gyges, my personal guard and minister, bears little resemblance to the idle rumors that have made the rounds concerning the episode. None of the versions I have heard comes even close to the truth. That is always the way it is: though fantasy and truth have one and the same heart, their faces are like day and night, like fire and water. There was no wager or any sort of exchange involved: it all happened quite spontaneously, on a sudden impulse of mine, the work of chance or a plot by some playful little god.

We had attended an interminable ceremony on the vast parade ground near the Palace, where vassal tribes, come to offer me tribute, deafened our ears with their brutish chants and blinded us with the dust raised by the acrobatic tricks of their horsemen. We also saw a pair of those sorcerers who cure ills with the ashes of corpses and a holy man who prayed by twirling around and around on his heels. The latter was impressive: impelled by the strength of his faith and the breathing exercises that accompanied his dance—a hoarse panting that grew louder and louder and appeared to be coming from his very guts—he turned into a human whirlwind and, at one point, the speed he attained was such that it caused him to vanish from our sight. When he again assumed corporeal form and ceased whirling, he was sweating like a war-horse after a cavalry charge and had the dull pallor and the dazed eyes of those who have seen a god, or a number of them.

My minister and I were speaking of the sorcerers and the holy man as we savored a cup of Greek wine, when good Gyges, with that wicked gleam that drink leaves in his eyes, suddenly lowered his voice and whispered to me:

"The Egyptian woman I've bought has the most beautiful backside that Providence has ever bestowed upon a woman. Her face is imperfect, her breasts are small, and she sweats excessively; but the abundance and generosity of her posterior more than compensate for all her defects. Something the mere memory of which dizzies my brain, Your Majesty."

"Show it to me and I'll show you another. We'll compare and decide which is better, Gyges."

I saw him lose his composure, blink, part his lips to speak, and yet say nothing. Did he believe that I was speaking in jest? Did he fear he had not heard right? My guard and minister knew very well who it was we were speaking of. I had made that proposal without thinking, but once it was made, an irksome little worm began to gnaw at my brain and rouse my anxiety.

"You haven't uttered a word, Gyges. What is troubling you?"

"I don't know what to say, sire. I'm disconcerted."

"So I see. Go on, give me your answer. Do you accept my offer?"

"Your Majesty knows that his desires are mine."

That was how it all began. We went first to his residence, and at the far end of the garden, where the steam baths are, as we sweated and his masseur rejuvenated our members, I scrutinized the Egyptian woman. A very tall woman, her face marred by those scars with which people of her race dedicate pubescent girls to their bloodthirsty god. She was already past childhood. But she was interesting and attractive, I grant. Her ebony skin shone amid the clouds of steam as though it had been varnished, and all her movements and gestures revealed an extraordinary hauteur. She showed not the slightest trace of that abject servility, so common in slaves, aimed at attaining the favor of their masters, but, rather, an elegant coldness. She did not understand our language, yet she immediately deciphered the instructions transmitted to her by her master through gestures. Once Gyges had indicated what it was we wanted to see, the woman, enveloping the two of us for a few seconds in her silken, scornful gaze, turned around, bent over, and lifted her tunic with both hands, offering us her backside. It was indeed notable, a veritable miracle in the eyes of anyone save the spouse of Lucrecia, the queen. Firm and spherical, gently curved, the skin hairless and fine-grained, with a blue sheen, over which one's gaze glided as over the sea. Bliss, and bliss likewise for my guard and minister, as the owner of such a sweet delight.

In order to fulfill my part of the offer, we were obliged to act with the greatest discretion. That episode with Atlas, the slave, had been deeply shocking to my wife, as I have already recounted: Lucrecia acquiesced because she satisfies my every whim. But I saw her so overcome with shame as Atlas and she did their best, to no avail, to act out the fantasy which I had woven that I swore to myself not to subject her to such a test again. Even now, when so long a time has passed since that episode, when there must be nothing left of Atlas but bones picked clean in the bottom of the stinking ravine teeming with vultures and hawks into which his remains were flung, the queen sometimes awakens at night, overcome with terror in my arms, for in her sleep the shadow of the Ethiopian has once again burst into flame on top of her.

Hence, this time I arranged matters so that my beloved would not know. That was my intention at least, though on reflection, delving into the chinks of my memory in search of what took place that night, I sometimes have my doubts.

I took Gyges through the little garden gate and introduced him into the apartments as the maidservants were disrobing Lucrecia and perfuming her and anointing her with the essences that it pleases me to smell and savor on her body. I suggested to my minister that he hide behind the draperies of the balcony and try not to move or make the slightest sound. From that coign, he had a perfect view of the splendid bed with carved corner posts, bedside steps, and red satin curtains, richly decorated with cushions, silks, and precious embroideries, where each night the queen and I staged our love matches. And I snuffed out all the lamp wicks, so that the room was lighted only by the crackling tongues of flame in the fireplace.

Lucrecia entered shortly thereafter, drifting in dressed in a filmy semitransparent tunic of white silk, with exquisitely delicate lacework at the wrists, neck, and hem. She was wearing a pearl necklace and a coif, and her feet were shod in felt slippers with high wooden platform soles and heels.

I kept her there before me for a fair time, feasting my eyes upon her and offering my good minister this spectacle fit for the gods. And as I contemplated her and thought of Gyges doing the same, that perverse complicity that united us suddenly made me burn with desire. Without a word I advanced upon her, pushed her onto the bed, and mounted her. As I caressed her, Gyges' bearded face appeared to me and the idea that he was watching us inflamed me even more, seasoning my pleasure with a bittersweet, piquant condiment hitherto unknown to me. And Lucrecia? Did she surmise that something was afoot? Did she know? Because I think I never felt her to be as spirited as she was that time, never so eager to take the initiative, to respond, never so bold at biting, kissing, embracing. Perhaps she sensed that, that night, it was not two of us but three who took our pleasure in that bedchamber turned a glowing red by candlelight and desire set aflame.

When, at dawn, as Lucrecia lay sleeping, I slipped out of bed and went on tiptoe to guide my guard and minister to the gate leading out of the garden, I found him shivering with cold and astonishment.

"You were right, Your Majesty," he stammered, ecstatic, tremulous. "I have seen it and it still seems to me that I merely dreamed it."

"Forget all about it this very minute and forever, Gyges," I ordered him. "I have granted you this privilege in a strange access of passion, without having expressly planned it, because of the esteem I have for you. But watch your tongue. I would not be pleased if this story were to become tavern gossip and marketplace tittle-tattle. I might regret having brought you here."

He swore to me that he would never say a word.

But he did. If not, how did there come to be so many stories about what happened? The various versions contradict one another, each of them more absurd and more untrue than the next. They reach our ears, and though they annoyed us in the beginning, they amuse us now. It is something that has come to be part of this little southern kingdom of that country which centuries later will go by the name of Turkey. Like its bone-dry mountains and its churlish subjects, like its wandering tribes, its falcons, and its bears. After all, I am not displeased at the idea that, once time has gone by, swallowing everything that now exists and surrounds me, the one thing to come down to future generations on the waters of the shipwreck of Lydia's history will be, round and solar, bountiful as spring, the croup of Lucrecia the queen, my wife.

Three.
The Wednesday
Ear Ritual

"They're like conch shells that bear within them, trapped in their mother-of-pearl labyrinth, the music of the sea," Don Rigoberto fantasized. His ears were large and prominent; both of them, but the left one in particular, tended to stand out from his head at the top, curving back on themselves, determined to capture for themselves only all the world's sounds. Though as a child he was ashamed of their size and their downturned form, he had learned to accept them. And now that he devoted one night a week to their care alone, he even felt proud of them. Because, moreover, by dint of careful and persistent experimenting, he had managed to get those graceless appendages to participate, along with the alacrity of his mouth and the efficacy of his sense of touch, in his nights of love. Lucrecia, too, was fond of them and, in private, paid them any number of pretty compliments. In certain phases of their conjugal cavalry skirmishes she affectionately referred to them as "my little Dumbos."

"Full-blown flowers, sensitive wing cases, auditoriums for music and dialogues," Don Rigoberto poeticized. With the aid of a magnifying glass, he carefully examined the cartilaginous edges of his left ear. Yes, the tiny tips of little hairs plucked out the previous Wednesday were showing again. There were three of them, asymmetrical, like the points defining the sides of a scalene triangle. He imagined the dark little tuft of hair that they would turn into if he let them grow, if he stopped rooting them out, and a fleeting sensation of nausea suddenly came over him. Hurriedly, with the dexterity stemming from constant practice, he grasped those hairy heads between the prongs of the tweezers and pulled them out, one after the other. The tingling sensation that accompanied the extirpation made a delicious hot-and-cold shiver run up his spine. It was as though Doña Lucrecia were there, kneeling, her even white teeth disentangling the kinky little ringlets of his pubis. The mere idea gave him a semi-erection. He reined it in immediately, imagining a hirsute woman, her ears clogged with clumps of matted hair and a pronounced mustache on her upper lip, in whose shadows drops of sweat were trembling. He then remembered the story that a colleague of his in the insurance business had recounted, that time, on returning from a vacation in the Caribbean: how the undisputed queen of a brothel in Santo Domingo was a big beefy mulatta with a startling hairy crest between her breasts. He tried to imagine Lucrecia with a similar attribute—a silken mane!—between her ivory breasts and was horrified. I have all sorts of prejudices when it comes to lovemaking, he confessed to himself. But for the moment he had no intention of giving up any of them. Hair was acceptable, it was a strong sexual seasoning, provided it was in the proper place. On a head or a mons veneris, welcome and indispensable; under the arms, tolerable perhaps, if only so as to have tried everything (it was apparently an obsession with Europeans); but on arms and legs, definitely out; and between the breasts, never!

He then proceeded to examine his left ear, with the aid of his convex shaving mirrors. No, no new little hairs had popped out in any of the angles, protuberances, and curves of his outer ear, except for those three musketeers whose presence he had spied, to his surprise, one fine day, some years ago now.

Tonight I shall not make love but hear it, he decided. That was possible; he had done so on other occasions and it amused Lucrecia, too, at least as part of the prolegomena. "Let me hear your breasts," he would murmur, and amorously plugging his wife's nipples, first one and then the other, into the hypersensitive cavern of his two ears—which they fit into as snugly as a foot into a moccasin—he would listen to them with his eyes closed, reverent and ecstatic, his mind worshipfully concentrated as at the Elevation of the Host, till he heard ascending to the earthy roughness of each button, from subterranean carnal depths, certain stifled cadences, the heavy breathing, perhaps, of her pores opening, the boiling, perhaps, of her excited blood.

He was removing the piliform excrescences from his right ear. All of a sudden he spied a stranger: the solitary little hair was swaying back and forth, disgustingly, in the center of his neatly turned earlobe. He pulled it out with a slight jerk, and before throwing it into the washbasin to be flushed down the drain, he examined it with distaste. Would new hairs keep appearing in his big ears in the years to come? In any event, he would never give up; even on his deathbed, had he strength left, he would go on destroying them (pruning them, rather?). After that, however, as his body lay lifeless, the intruders could sprout at will, grow, blemish his corpse. The same would be true of his fingernails. Don Rigoberto told himself that this depressing perspective was an irrefutable argument in favor of cremation. Yes, fire would prevent posthumous imperfection. The flames would cause him to disappear while he was still perfect, thereby frustrating the worms. The thought came as a relief to him.

As he rolled little balls of cotton around the tips of the tweezers and wet them with soap and water so as to clean out the wax that had accumulated inside his ear, he anticipated what those clean funnels would soon be hearing as they descended from his wife's breasts to her navel. They need make no special effort there to surprise Lucrecia's secret music, for a veritable symphony of sounds, liquid and solid, prolonged and brief, diffuse and clear, would immediately reveal their hidden life to him. He looked forward with gratitude to how deeply he would be moved to perceive, thanks to those organs which he was now scraping clean with meticulous care and affection, ridding them of the oily film that formed on them every so often, something of the secret existence of her body: glands, muscles, blood vessels, hair follicles, membranes, tissues, filaments, ducts, tubes, all that rich and subtle biological orography that lay beneath the smooth epidermis of Lucrecia's belly. I love everything that exists on the inside or the outside of her, he thought. Because everything about her is—or can be—erogenous.

He was not exaggerating, carried away by the tenderness that her sudden appearance in his fantasies always gave rise to. No, absolutely not. For thanks to his unyielding perseverance, he had managed to fall in love with the whole and with each one of the parts of his wife, to love, separately and together, all the components of that cellular universe. He knew himself to be capable of responding erotically, with a prompt, robust erection, to the stimulus of any of its infinite ingredients, including the meanest and humblest, including what—to the ordinary hominid—was most inconceivable and most repellent. "Here lies Don Rigoberto, who contrived to love the epigastrium of his spouse as much as her vulva or her tongue," he philosophically projected as a fitting epitaph on the marble of his tomb. Would that mortuary motto be a lie? Not in the slightest. He thought of how impassioned he would become, very shortly, when the sound of muffled aqueous displacements reached his ears, avidly flattened against her soft stomach, and at this moment he could already hear the lively burbling of that flatus, the joyous cracking of a fart, the gargle and yawn of her vagina, or the languid stretching of her serpentine intestine. And he could already hear himself whispering, blind with love and lust, the phrases with which it was his habit to render his wife homage as he caressed her. "Those little noises, too, are you, Lucrecia; they are your characteristic harmony, your resounding person." He was certain that he could immediately recognize them, distinguish them from the sounds produced by the abdomen of any other woman. It was a hypothesis that he would not have the opportunity to verify, since he would never embark upon the experiment of hearing love with any other woman. Why would he do such a thing? Wasn't Lucrecia an ocean of unfathomable depths that he, the lover-diver, would never have done with exploring? "I love you," he murmured, feeling once again the dawn of an erection. He conjured it away with a fillip of his finger, which, besides making him double over, brought on a fit of laughter. "He who laughs by himself is recalling his perversities!" he heard his wife admonishing him from the bedroom. Ah, if only Lucrecia knew what he was laughing about.

To hear her voice, to confirm her presence close at hand, and her existence, filled him with happiness. "Happiness exists," he repeated to himself, as he did every night. Yes, provided one sought it where it was possible. In one's own body and in that of one's beloved, for instance; by oneself and in the bathroom; for hours or minutes on a bed shared with the being so ardently desired. Because happiness was temporal, individual, in exceptional circumstances twofold, on extremely rare occasions tripartite, and never collective, civic. It was hidden, a pearl in its seashell, in certain rites or ceremonial duties that offered human beings brief flashes and optical illusions of perfection. One had to be content with these crumbs so as not to live at the mercy of anxiety and despair, slapping at the impossible. Happiness lies hidden in the hollow of my ears, he thought, in a mellow mood.

He had finished cleaning the canals of both ears and there, beneath his gaze, were the little balls of moist cotton, impregnated with the oily yellow humor he had just removed from them. The one thing left to do now was to dry them, so that no dirt would crystallize in those drops of water before they evaporated. Once again he rolled two little balls of cotton around the tip of the tweezers and scrubbed the canals so gently that he appeared to be massaging or caressing them. He then threw the little balls of cotton in the toilet and pulled the chain. He cleaned the pair of tweezers and put it away in his wife's little aloeswood kit.

He carefully inspected his ears one last time in the mirror. He felt satisfied, cheerful, and resolute. There those cartilaginous cones were, clean outside and in, ready to bend over to listen, respectfully and incontinently, to the body of his beloved.

Four.
Eyes Like Fireflies

"Turning forty isn't so terrible, after all," Doña Lucrecia thought, stretching lazily in the darkened bedroom. She felt young, beautiful, and happy. Did happiness exist, then? Rigoberto said it did, "sometimes, for the two of us." Wasn't it a hollow word, a state that only fools attained? Her husband loved her, he proved it to her in tender, thoughtful little ways each day and sought her favors with youthful ardor nearly every night. Ever since they had decided to marry, four months before, he too seemed to have grown younger. The fears that had kept her from taking that step for so long—her first marriage had been a disaster and the divorce a nightmarish torment at the hands of money-grubbing shysters—had vanished. From the very outset, she had taken over her new household with the greatest assurance. The first thing she did was to redecorate all the rooms, so that nothing would summon up remembrances of Rigoberto's late wife, and she now ran the house with a sure hand, as though she had always been the mistress of it. Only the cook, who had been there before she came, showed a certain hostility toward her, and she had had to replace her. The other servants got along very well with her. Justiniana especially; promoted by Doña Lucrecia to the status of personal maid, she turned out to be a real find: efficient, smart, extremely clean, and possessed of unfailing devotion.

But the greatest success was her relationship with the little boy. He had been her greatest concern at one time, something she had believed to be an insurmountable obstacle. A stepson, Lucrecia, she would think whenever Rigoberto insisted that they put an end to their semiclandestine affair and get married without further ado. It's never going to work. That child is always going to hate you. He'll make life impossible for you, and sooner or later you'll end up hating him as well. When has a couple ever been happy when other people's children enter the picture?

But that wasn't how it had turned out at all. Alfonsito adored her. Yes, that was the right word. Perhaps a little too much, in fact. Doña Lucrecia stretched between the warm sheets again, coiling and uncoiling like a lazying serpent. Hadn't he finished first in his class to please her? She remembered his flushed face, the triumph in his sky-blue eyes when he had handed her his report card:

"Here's your birthday present, stepmother. May I give you a kiss?"

"Of course, Fonchito. Ten, if you like."

He was forever asking her for kisses and giving them to her, with an excitement that, at times, gave her misgivings. Could the child really be that fond of her? Yes, she had won him over with all those presents, all that pampering, from the moment she had first set foot in the house. Or, as Rigoberto fantasized, fanning his desire in the midst of his nocturnal labors, was Alfonsito awakening to sexual life and had circumstances entrusted her with the role of inspirer? "What nonsense, Rigoberto. When he's still just a little boy, when he's just made his First Communion. What absurd notions you have sometimes."

But even though she would never confess aloud to such a thing, least of all in her husband's presence, when she was by herself, as she was now, Doña Lucrecia wondered whether the boy was not, in fact, discovering desire, the nascent poetry of the body, using her as a stimulus. Alfonsito's attitude intrigued her: it seemed so innocent yet at the same time so ambiguous. She remembered then—it was an incident dating from her adolescence that she never forgot—the chance pattern she saw the graceful little feet of a seagull trace in the sand at the

Yacht Club; she went closer to get a better look, expecting to come upon an abstract form, a labyrinth of straight lines and curves, and what she saw reminded her, rather, of a big, humpbacked penis! Was Foncho aware that when he threw his arms around her neck the way he did, when he gave her those lingering kisses, seeking her lips, he was going beyond the bounds of the permissible? Impossible to know. The child had such a candid, such a gentle gaze, that it seemed impossible to Doña Lucrecia that the small blond head of this exquisite beauty posing as a shepherd in the Christmas tableaux at the Santa María School for Boys could harbor dirty, scabrous thoughts.

"Dirty thoughts," she whispered, her mouth against the pillow, "scabrous thoughts. Ha-ha!" She felt in fine spirits, and a delicious warmth was coursing through her veins, as though her blood had been transubstantiated into mulled wine. No, Fonchito couldn't have any intimation that he was playing with fire; those effusions were doubtless prompted by a vague instinct, an unconscious tropism. They were dangerous games, nonetheless, weren't they, Lucrecia? Because when she saw him, just a little boy still, kneeling on the floor, contemplating her as though his stepmother had just descended from Paradise, or when his little arms and his frail body clung to her, and his lips, so thin as to be nearly invisible, glued themselves to her cheeks and slid down to graze hers—she had never permitted them to linger there for more than a second—Doña Lucrecia could not help feeling at times a sudden sharp stab of excitement, a steamy breath of desire. "You're the one who has dirty, scabrous thoughts, Lucrecia," she murmured, hugging the mattress with her eyes closed. Would she one day become a hot-to-trot older woman, like some of her bridge cronies? Was that what was meant by the devil at midday, the passion of women of a certain age? Calm yourself, remember that you've been a grass widow for two days—Rigoberto, off on a business trip, some sort of deal having to do with insurance, wouldn't be back till Sunday—and no more of this lolling about in bed. On your feet, you lazy creature! Struggling to shake off her pleasant drowsiness, she picked up the intercom and ordered Justiniana to bring her breakfast upstairs.

The girl entered the room five minutes later, with Doña Lucrecia's breakfast on a tray, and her mail and the morning newspapers. She opened the curtains, and the humid, dreary gray light of September in Lima invaded the room. How grim winter is, Doña Lucrecia thought. And she dreamed of the summer sun, the burning sands of the beaches of Paracas, and the salty caress of the sea on her skin. So far off still! Justiniana placed the tray on her lap and plumped up the pillows to make a backrest. She was a slender woman, dark-skinned and kinky-haired, with bright sparkling eyes and a melodious voice.

"There's something I don't know how to tell you, señora," she murmured, a tragicomic expression on her face, as she handed Doña Lucrecia her dressing gown and placed her mules at the foot of the bed.

"Well, you must tell me now, because you've whetted my appetite," Doña Lucrecia said as she bit into a slice of toast and took a sip of tea without sugar or cream. "What's happened?"

"I'm ashamed to say, señora."

Doña Lucrecia, amused, looked at her closely. She was a young woman, and beneath the blue apron of her uniform was the merest hint of the supple curves of her slender, resilient body. What did she look like when her husband made love to her? She was married to a doorman at a restaurant, a tall black as well built as an athlete, who brought her to the house every morning. Doña Lucrecia had advised her not to complicate her life by having children while she was still so young, and had personally taken her to her own doctor to get her a prescription for the pill.

"Another fight between the cook and Saturnino?"

"No, it has to do with little Alfonso." Justiniana lowered her voice as though the boy could hear her from his far-off school, and pretended to be more embarrassed than she really was. "The thing is, last night I caught him . . . But please don't tell him, señora. If Fonchito finds out I told you, he'll kill me."

These affectations of modesty and exaggerated

fears with which Justiniana always embroidered whatever she was saying amused Doña Lucrecia.

"Where did you catch him? Doing what?"

"Spying on you, señora."

Some instinct warned Doña Lucrecia of what she was about to hear and put her on her guard. Justiniana was pointing to the bathroom ceiling and seemed genuinely embarrassed now.

"He could have fallen down into the garden and might even have killed himself," she whispered, rolling her eyes. "That's why I'm telling you, señora. When I scolded him, he told me it wasn't the first time. He'd climbed up onto the roof lots of times. To spy on you."

"What's that you're telling me?"

"Just what you heard," the child answered defiantly, almost heroically. "And I'll go on doing it even if I slip and fall and kill myself, if you want to know the truth."

"You've lost your mind, Fonchito. That's very bad; it's just not right. What would Don Rigoberto say if he found out that you spy on your stepmother while she's taking a bath? He'd be terribly angry; he'd give you a thrashing. And what's more, you might kill yourself. Just think how high up it is."

"I don't care," the boy said, a determined gleam in his eye. But he calmed down immediately and, shrugging his shoulders, added meekly: "Even though my papa beats me, Justita. So, are you going to tell on me?"

"I won't say a word to him if you promise me you won't ever climb up here again."

"I can't promise you that, Justita," the boy said regretfully. "I don't make promises I'm not going to keep."

"Aren't you making all this up with that tropical imagination of yours?" Doña Lucrecia stammered. Ought she to laugh, lose her temper?

"I hesitated a long time before working up my courage to tell you, señora. Because I love Fonchito so dearly; he's such a good boy. But the thing is, he could kill himself climbing up on that roof, I swear it."

Doña Lucrecia tried in vain to imagine him up there, crouching like a wild animal, watching her.

"I just can't bring myself to believe it. So polite, so well mannered. I just can't see him doing a thing like that."

"It's because Fonchito has fallen in love with you, señora." The girl sighed, clapping a hand over her mouth and smiling. "Don't tell me you didn't know, because I don't believe it."

"What nonsense you're talking, Justiniana."

"Is there such a thing as a right age for love, señora? There are youngsters who first fall in love at Fonchito's age. And what's more, he's smart as a whip, no matter what he's up to. If only you'd heard what he told me, you'd be dumbfounded. Left with your mouth hanging open. The way I was."

"What's this story you're making up now, you silly girl?"

"It's just the way I'm telling you, Justita. When she takes off her dressing gown and gets into the tubful of foam, I can't tell you what I feel. She's so pretty, so very pretty. It's as though I'm watching a movie, I tell you. It's as though—it's something I just can't explain to you. Could that be why I cry, do you think?"

Doña Lucrecia chose to burst out laughing. The maidservant felt more sure of herself and smiled, too, a look of complicity on her face.

"I believe only a tenth of what you're telling me," Doña Lucrecia finally said, climbing out of bed. "But even so, something has to be done about that boy. Cut these games off at their very root, and do so immediately."

"Please don't tell the señor," Justiniana begged her, in fear and trembling. "He'd be very angry and might give him a thrashing. Fonchito doesn't have the least idea he's doing something bad. I give you my word he doesn't. He's like a little angel; he doesn't know good from evil."

"I can't tell Rigoberto, no, of course not," Doña Lucrecia agreed, thinking aloud. "But this foolishness must be brought to an end. Immediately, though I don't know how."

She felt apprehensive and uneasy, irritated at the boy, the maidservant, and herself. What should she do? Have a word with Fonchito and reprimand him? Threaten to tell Rigoberto the whole story? What would his reaction be? Would he be hurt, feel betrayed? Would the love he now felt for her suddenly turn into hatred?

Soaping herself, she fondled her big strong breasts, the erect nipples, and her still-graceful waist, from which the ample curves of her hips opened out, like two halves of a fruit, and her thighs, her buttocks, her armpits with the hair removed, and her long smooth neck with one solitary mole. "I shall never grow old," she prayed, as she did each morning at her bath. "Even if it means having to sell my soul or anything else. I shall never be ugly or miserable. I shall die beautiful and happy." Don Rigoberto had convinced her that saying, repeating, and believing these things would make them come true. "Sympathetic magic, my love." Lucrecia smiled: her husband might be a little eccentric, but, in all truth, a woman never tired of a man like that.

All the rest of the day, as she gave orders to the servants, went shopping, visited a woman friend, lunched, made and received phone calls, she wondered what to do with the child. If she gave his secret away to Rigoberto, he would turn into her enemy and then the old premonition of a domestic hell would become a reality. Perhaps the most sensible thing to do was to forget Justiniana's revelation and, adopting a cool aloofness, gradually undermine the fantasies the boy had woven around her, no doubt only half aware that that was what they were. Yes, that was the prudent thing to do: say nothing, and, little by little, distance herself from him.

That afternoon, when Alfonsito, back from school, came to kiss her, she quickly turned her cheek away and buried herself in the magazine she was leafing through, without asking him how his classes had gone or if he had homework for the next day. Out of the corner of her eye, she saw his little face pucker up in a tearful pout. But she was not moved and that night she let him eat his dinner alone, without coming downstairs to keep him company as she often did (she rarely ate dinner herself). Rigoberto phoned her a little later, from Trujillo. All his business deals had gone well and he missed her lots. He would miss her even more that night, in his dreary room in the Hotel de Turistas. Nothing new there at home? No, nothing. Take good care of yourself, darling. Doña Lucrecia listened to a bit of music, alone in her room, and when the child came to bid her good night, she coldly bade him the same. Shortly thereafter, she told Justiniana to prepare the bubble bath she always took before going to bed.

As the girl drew the bathwater and she undressed, the feeling of apprehension that had dogged her footsteps all day came to the fore again, much stronger now. Had she done the right thing by treating Fonchito as she had? Despite herself, it pained her to remember the look of hurt and surprise on his little face. But wasn't that the only way to put a stop to childish behavior that threatened to become dangerous?

She was half asleep in the tub, immersed up to her neck, stirring the swirls of soap bubbles with a hand or a foot, when Justiniana knocked on the door: might she come in, señora? Doña Lucrecia watched her approach, a towel in one hand and a dressing gown in the other, with a frightened look on her face. She realized immediately what the girl was about to whisper to her: "Fonchito is up there, señora." She nodded and with an imperious wave of her hand ordered Justiniana out of the room.

She lay in the water without moving for a long time, carefully not looking up. Ought she to look? Should she point her finger at him? Cry out, call him names? She could hear the clatter behind the dark glass cupola overhead; see in her mind's eye the little kneeling figure, his fright, his feeling of shame. She could hear his strident scream, see him break into a run. He would slip, fall into the garden with the roar of a rocket exploding. The sudden thud of his little body as it hit the balustrade, flattened the croton hedge, caught in the witchy-fingered branches of the datura would reach her ears. "Make an effort, control yourself," she said to herself, clenching her teeth. "Don't create a scandal. Keep clear, above all, of something that might end in tragedy."

She was trembling with anger from head to foot and her teeth were chattering, as though she were chilled to the bone. Suddenly she rose to her feet. Not covering herself with the towel, not cowering so that those invisible little eyes would have no more than an imperfect, fleeting vision of her body. No, quite the contrary; she stood up on tiptoe, parting her legs, and before emerging from her bath she stretched, revealing herself generously, obscenely, as she removed her plastic bath cap and loosed her long hair with a toss of her head. And on stepping out of the bathtub, instead of donning her dressing gown immediately, she stood there naked, her body gleaming with tiny drops of water, tense, daring, furious. She dried herself very slowly, limb by limb, rubbing the towel over her skin again and again, leaning to one side, bending over, halting at times as though distracted by a sudden idea, in a posture of indecent abandon, or contemplating herself carefully in the mirror. And with the same lingering, maniacal care she then rubbed her body with moisturizing lotions. And as she thus displayed herself before the invisible observer, her heart pulsed with wrath. What are you doing, Lucrecia? What is the meaning of these affected poses, Lucrecia? But she went on exposing herself, as she had never done before to anyone, not even to Don Rigoberto, moving from one side of the bathroom to the other at a slow, deliberate pace, naked, as she brushed her hair and her teeth and sprayed herself with cologne. As she played the leading role in this improvised spectacle, she had the presentiment that what she was

doing was also a subtle way of punishing the precocious libertine crouched in the darkness up above,
with images of an intimacy that would shatter, once
and for all, that innocence that served him as an
excuse for his boldness.

When she climbed into bed, she was still trembling. She lay there for a long time, unable to sleep,
missing Rigoberto. She felt thoroughly displeased
with what she had done; she positively detested the
boy and forced herself not to divine the meaning of
those hot flashes that, from time to time, electrified
her nipples. What's happened to you, woman? She
did not recognize herself. Could it be because she'd
turned forty? Or a consequence of those nocturnal
fantasies and bizarre caprices of her husband's? But
it was all Alfonsito's fault. That child is corrupting
me, she thought, disconcerted.

When, finally, she managed to drop off to sleep,
she had a voluptuous dream that seemed to bring
to life one of those etchings in Don Rigoberto's secret collection that he and she were in the habit of
contemplating and commenting upon together at
night, seeking inspiration for their love.

Five.

Diana

after Her Bath

That one, the one on the left, is me, Diana Lucrecia. Yes, me, the goddess of the oak tree and of forests, of fertility and childbirth, the goddess of the chase. The Greeks call me Artemis. I am related to the Moon and Apollo is my brother. Among my worshippers are countless women and common folk. There are temples in my honor scattered throughout the wilds of the Empire. On my right, bending over, gazing at my foot, is Justiniana, my favorite. We have just bathed, and are about to make love.

The hare, the partridges, the pheasant I bagged at dawn this morning, with arrows that, drawn from the game and cleaned by Justiniana, have been replaced in their quiver. The hounds are mere decoration; I rarely use them when I hunt. Never, in any event, to retrieve delicate prey such as today's, since their jaws mangle it so badly it becomes unfit to eat.

Tonight we shall eat the tender, tasty flesh of these animals, seasoned with exotic spices, and drink Capua wine, till we fall back exhausted. I know how to enjoy myself. It is an aptitude that I have been continually perfecting, throughout time and history, and I maintain, without boasting, that in this domain I have attained wisdom. By that I mean: the art of sipping the nectar of pleasure from every fruit—even those gone rotten—that life offers.

The main character is not in the picture. Or rather, he is not in sight. He is there in the background, hidden in the shady grove, spying on us. With his beautiful wide-open eyes the color of dawn in the south and his round face flushed with desire, he is surely there, squatting on his heels in a trance, adoring me. With his blond curls entangled in the branches of the bower and his little pale-skinned member raised on high like a banner, drinking us in and devouring us with the fantasy of an innocent child, he is surely there. Knowing that this delights us and adds zest to our sport. He is neither a god nor a little animal, but a member of the human species. He tends goats and plays the panpipes. He is called Foncín.

Justiniana discovered him, on the Ides of August, as I was tracking a stag through the forest. The little goatherd followed me, enthralled, tripping and stumbling, not taking his eyes off me for a single instant. My favorite says that when he saw me, drawn up to my full height, a ray of sunlight setting

François Boucher, *Diana at the Bath* (1742),
oil on canvas, The Louvre, Paris

my hair afire and kindling a wild gleam in the pupils of my eyes, as all the muscles of my body tensed to let loose the arrow, the little darling burst into tears. She drew nearer to console him, whereupon she saw that the child was weeping for joy.

"I don't know what's happening to me," he confessed to her, his cheeks wet with tears, "but every time the lady appears in the forest, the leaves of the trees turn into morning stars and all the flowers burst into song. An ardent spirit steals within me and heats my blood. I see her and it is as if, poised motionless on the ground, I suddenly turned into a bird and began to fly."

"Despite his tender years, the form of your body has inspired in him the language of love," Justiniana philosophized, recounting the episode to me. "Your beauty holds him spellbound, as the rattlesnake fascinates the hummingbird. Have pity on him, Diana Lucrecia. Why don't we play games with the little goatherd? By amusing him, we shall amuse ourselves as well."

And so it was. A born pleasure-seeker just as I am, and perhaps even more so, Justiniana is never mistaken in matters concerning sensual enjoyment. It is what delights me about her, even more than her luxuriant hips or the silky down of her pubis, so deliciously tickling to the palate: her swift imagination and her unfailing, instinctive recognition, amid the sound and fury of this world, of the sources of diversion and pleasure.

From that moment on, we have played with him, and although quite some time has passed, our sport is so agreeable we never tire of it. Each day is more diverting than the day before, adding novelty and good humor to existence.

Along with his physical charms of a virile little god, Foncín is graced with another that is spiritual: timidity. The two or three attempts I have made to approach him so as to speak to him have been in vain. He pales and, a shy little musk deer, breaks into a run, fading into the network of branches as if by magic. He has intimated to Justiniana that the mere idea, not of touching me, but simply of being close to me, of having me look into his eyes and speak to him, dizzies him, devastates him. "A lady such as that is untouchable," he has told her. "I know that if I approach her, her beauty will consume me as the sun of Libya consumes the butterfly."

Hence, we play our games in secret. Each of them different, a simulacrum like those theatrical dramas—so pleasing to the Greeks, those sentimentalists—wherein gods and mortals mingle in order to suffer and kill each other. Justiniana, pretending to be his accomplice and not mine—in point of fact, that clever creature is the accomplice of us both, and above all of herself—installs the little goatherd in a rocky spot, close by the cavern where I shall spend the night. And then, by the light of the fire with its reddish tongues of flame, she disrobes me and anoints my body with the honey of the gentle bees of Sicily. It is a Lacedaemonian formula for keeping the body taut and lustrous, and what is more, it rouses one's senses. As she leans down over me, rubs my limbs, moves them, and offers them to the curious gaze of my chaste admirer, I half close my eyes. As I descend through the tunnel of sensation and quiver in delicious little spasms, I divine the presence of Foncín. More than that: I see him, I smell him, I caress him, I press him to my bosom and make him disappear within me, with no need to touch him. It makes my ecstasy the keener to know that as I near climax beneath the diligent hands of my favorite, he is doing the same, at the pace I set, along with me. His innocent little body, glistening with sweat as he watches me and takes his pleasure by watching me, contributes a note of tenderness that subtly shades and sweetens mine.

Thus, hidden from me by Justiniana amid the forest greenery, the little goatherd has seen me fall asleep and waken, throw the javelin and the dart, dress and undress myself. He has seen me squat down on two stones and watched my pale gold urine flow into a transparent little brook, whereupon he will immediately hasten downstream to drink from it. He has seen me decapitate geese and eviscerate doves so as to offer their blood to the gods and read in their entrails the hidden mysteries of the future. He has seen me caress and sate myself and caress and sate my favorite, and he has seen Justiniana and me, immersed in the stream, drink the crystalline water of the cascade, each from the mouth of the other, savoring our mingled saliva, our juices, and our sweat. There is no exercise or function, no wanton ritual of body or soul that we have not performed for him, the privileged freeholder enjoying our privacy from his errant hiding places. He is our buffoon; but he is also our master. He is in our service and we in his. Without having ever touched each other or exchanged a single word, we have brought each other to the heights of rapture countless times and it is not inexact to say that, despite the unbridgeable abyss that our different natures and ages open up between him and me, we are more nearly one than the most impassioned pair of lovers.

Now, at this very moment, Justiniana and I are going to perform for him, and Foncín, simply by remaining there where he is, between the stone wall and the grove, will also perform for the two of us.

In a word, this eternal immobility will come to life and be time, history. The hounds will bay, the copse will trill, the water of the river will sing its way amid the pebbles and the rushes, and the full-crowned clouds will drift eastward, driven by the same playful little breeze that will ruffle the madcap curls of my favorite. She will move, will bend down, and her little vermilion-lipped mouth will kiss my foot and suck each one of my toes as one sucks lemons and limes on sultry summer afternoons. Soon our limbs will be intertwined, as we gambol on the whispering silk of the blue coverlet, given over to the intoxication from which life springs. The hounds will circle us, breathing on us the hot vapor of their eager maws, and perhaps lick us excitedly. The grove will hear us sigh as we swoon and, then, each mortally wounded, let out a sudden cry. An instant later it will hear us laughing in boisterous jest. And it will see us slowly drowse off into a peaceful sleep, our limbs still intertwined.

It is then quite possible that, on seeing us prisoners of the god Hypnos, the witness of our poses, taking infinite precautions so as not to awaken us with his soft footfalls, will abandon his refuge and come to contemplate us from the edge of the blue coverlet.

There he will be and there we will be, motionless once again, in another eternal instant. Foncín, his brow pale and his cheeks blushing, his eyes wide open in astonishment and gratitude, a little thread of saliva dangling from his tender mouth. The two of us, perfectly commingled, breathing in unison, with the fulfilled look of women who know how to be happy. There the three of us will be, calm, patient, awaiting the artist of the future who, roused by desire, will imprison us in dreams and, pinning us to the canvas with his brush, will believe that he is inventing us.

Six.
Don Rigoberto's
Ablutions

Don Rigoberto entered the bathroom, bolted the door, and sighed. Instantly, a pleasing and gratifying sensation, of relief and expectation, came over him: in this solitary half hour he would be happy. He was happy every night, at times more, at others less, but the punctilious ritual that he had been perfecting down through the years, like an artist who polishes and hammers home each detail of his masterpiece, never failed to produce its miraculous effect: relaxing him, reconciling him with his fellows, rejuvenating him, raising his spirits. Each time, he left the bathroom with the feeling that, despite everything, life was worth living. He had, therefore, never once neglected to perform it, ever since—how long ago had it been?—he had had the idea of transforming what for ordinary mortals was a routine that they went through with the mindlessness of machines—

brushing their teeth, drying themselves, et cetera into an artful task that made of him, if only momentarily, a perfect being.

In his youth he had been a fervent militant in Catholic Action and dreamed of changing the world. He soon realized that, like all collective ideals, that particular one was an impossible dream, doomed to failure. His practical turn of mind led him not to waste his time waging battles that sooner or later he was bound to lose. He then conjectured that, as an ideal, perfection was perhaps possible for the isolated individual, if restricted to a limited sphere in space (cleanliness or corporeal sanctity, for example, or the practice of eroticism) and in time (ablutions and nocturnal emissions before going to sleep).

He removed his bathrobe, hung it on the back of the door, and, naked except for his house slippers, sat down on the toilet, separated from the rest of the bathroom by a lacquered screen with little dancing sky-blue figures. His stomach was a Swiss watch: disciplined and punctual, it always emptied itself at this particular time, totally and effortlessly, as though happy to rid itself of the policies and the detritus of the day's business. Ever since, in the most secret decision of his life—so secret that probably not even Lucrecia would ever be privy to it in its entirety—he had resolved to be perfect for a brief fragment of each day, and once he had worked out this ceremony, he had never again experienced asphyxiating attacks of constipation or demoralizing diarrhea.

Don Rigoberto half closed his eyes and strained, just a little. That was all it took: he immediately felt the beneficent tickle in his rectum and the sensation that, there inside, in the hollows of his lower belly, something obedient to his will was about to depart and was already wriggling its way down that passage which, in order to make its exit easier, was widening. His anus, in turn, had begun to dilate in anticipation, preparing itself to complete the expulsion of the expelled, whereupon it would shut itself up tight and pout, with its thousand little puckers, as though mocking: "You're gone, you rascal you, and can't ever return."

Don Rigoberto gave a satisfied smile. Shitting, defecating, excreting: synonyms for sexual pleasure? he thought. Of course. Why not? Provided it was done slowly, savoring the task, without the least hurry, taking one's time, imparting to the muscles of the colon a gentle, sustained quivering. It was a matter not of pushing but of guiding, of accompanying, of graciously escorting the gliding of the offerings toward the exit. Don Rigoberto sighed once again, his five senses absorbed in what was happening inside his body. He could almost see the spectacle: those expansions and retractions, those juices and masses in action, all of them in warm corporeal shadow and in a silence interrupted every so often by muffled gargles or the joyful broone of a mighty fart. He heard, finally, the discreet splash with which the first offering invited to leave his bowels plopped—was it floating, was it sinking?—into the water of the toilet bowl. Three or four more would fall. Eight was his Olympic record, the consequence of an extravagant lunch, with murderous mixtures of fats, sugars, and starches washed down with wines and spirits. As a general rule he evacuated five offerings; once the fifth was gone, after a few seconds' pause to give muscles, intestines, anus, rectum, due time to assume their orthodox positions once again, there invaded him that intimate rejoicing at a duty fulfilled and a goal attained, that same feeling of spiritual cleanliness that had once upon a time possessed him as a schoolboy at La Recoleta, after he had confessed his sins and done the penance assigned him by the father confessor.

But cleaning out one's belly is a much less dubious proposition than cleaning out one's soul, he thought. His stomach was clean now, no doubt about it. He spread his legs, leaned his head down and looked: those drab brown cylinders, half submerged in the green porcelain bowl, were proof. What penitent was able, as he was now, to see and (if he so desired) to touch the pestilential filth that repentance, confession, penance, and God's mercy drew out of the soul? When he was a practicing believer—he was now only the latter—the suspicion had never left him that, despite confession, however meticulously detailed, a certain quantity of filth remained stuck to the walls of his soul, a few stubborn, rebellious stains that penance was unable to remove.

It was, moreover, a feeling he had sometimes had, though far less strong and unaccompanied by anxiety, ever since he had read in a magazine how young novices in a Buddhist monastery in India purified their intestines. The operation involved three gymnastic exercises, a length of rope, and a basin for the evacuated stools. It had the simplicity and the clarity of perfect objects and acts, such as the circle and coitus. The author of the text, a Belgian professor of yoga, had practiced with them for forty days in order to master the technique. The description of the three exercises whereby the novices hastened evacuation was not clear enough, however, to allow one to picture the ritual in detail and imitate it. The professor of yoga guaranteed that by means of those three flexions, torsions, and gyrations the stomach dissolved all the impurities and remains of the (vegetarian) diet to which the novices were subjected. Once this first stage of purification of their bellies was completed, the youngsters—with a certain melancholy, Don Rigoberto imagined their shaved skulls and their austere little bodies covered by tunics the color of saffron or perhaps snow— proceeded to assume the proper posture: supple, pliant, leaning to one side, legs slightly apart and the soles of their feet firmly planted on the ground so as not to move a single millimeter, as their

bodioo ophidiano olowly owallowing the intormin
able little worm—absorbed, thanks to peristaltic
contractions, that rope which, coiling and uncoiling,
advancing calmly and inexorably through the moist
intestinal labyrinth, irresistibly pushed downward
all those leftovers, remains, adhesions, minutiae,
and excrescences that the emigrant oblations left
behind.

They purify themselves the way someone reams
out a rifle, he thought, filled once more with envy.
He imagined the dirty little head of the rope coming
back into the world by way of the little Quevedo-
esque eye of the ass, after having traversed and
cleaned out all those dark, tortuous inner recesses,
and he could see it come out and fall into the basin
like a crumpled carnival streamer. There it would
remain, of no use to anyone, along with the last
impurities that its presence had evacuated, ready for
the funeral pyre. How good those youngsters must
feel! How weightless! How free of all pollution! He
would never be able to follow their example, at least
as far as that experience was concerned. But Don
Rigoberto was certain that, if they left him far behind
when it came to the technique of sterilizing the bowels, in every other respect his ritual of bodily cleanliness was infinitely more scrupulous and technically
exacting than that of those exotic practitioners.

He gave one last push, discreet and soundless,
just in case. Could that anecdote by any chance be
true—the one that had it that the textual scholar

Don Marcelino Menéndez y Pelayo, who suffered from chronic constipation, spent a good part of his life, in his house in Santander, sitting on the toilet, straining? People had assured Don Rigoberto that in the house of the celebrated historian, poet, and critic, now a museum, the visiting tourist could contemplate the portable writing desk that Don Marcelino had had made to order for him so as not to be obliged to break off his research and his elegantly penned writings as he struggled against his mean, stingy belly, determined not to give up the fecal filth deposited there by heavy, hearty Spanish viands. It touched Don Rigoberto to imagine that robust intellectual, of such untroubled brow and such firm religious beliefs, shut up in his private water closet, perhaps bundled up in a thick plaid lap robe to withstand the freezing mountain cold, straining and straining for hours at a time as, undaunted, he went on digging about in old folio volumes and dusty incunabula of the history of Spain in his search for heterodoxies, impieties, schisms, blasphemies, and doctrinal follies to be catalogued.

He wiped himself with four small squares of folded tissue and flushed the toilet. He went over to the bidet, sat down, filled it with warm water, and meticulously soaped his anus, phallus, testicles, pubis, crotch, and buttocks. Then he rinsed himself off and dried himself with a clean towel.

Today was Tuesday, foot day. He had divided the week up among different organs and members:

Monday, hands; Wednesday, ears; Thursday, nose; Friday, hair; Saturday, eyes; and Sunday, skin. This was the variable element of the nocturnal ritual, what left it open to possible change and reformation. Concentrating each night on just one area of his body allowed him to carry out the task of cleaning it and preserving it with greater thoroughness and attention to detail; and by so doing, to know and to love it more. With each individual organ and area the master of his labors for one day, perfect impartiality with regard to the care of the whole was assured: there were no favoritisms, no postponements, no odious hierarchies with respect to the overall treatment and detailed consideration of part and whole. He thought: My body is that impossibility: an egalitarian society.

He filled the washbasin with warm water and, installing himself on the toilet-seat cover, soaked his feet for quite some time so as to reduce the swelling in his heels, the soles of his feet, his toes, ankles, and insteps, and soften them. He did not have bunions or flat feet, though his instep, it was quite true, was unusually high. No matter; that was a minor deformity, imperceptible to anyone who did not subject his feet to clinical examination. As for size, proportion, conformation of toes and toenails, nomenclature and anatomy of the bones, everything appeared to be more or less normal. The danger lay in the corns and calluses that, every so often, did their best to make them look ugly. But he knew how to cut the evil off at the root, always in good time.

He had the pumice stone at the ready. He began with the left foot. At the upper edge of the heel, there where the friction from his shoe was greatest, an adventitious, horny growth had already begun to form, which felt to his fingertips as rough as an unplastered wall. By rubbing the pumice stone back and forth over it repeatedly, he gradually wore it down till there was nothing left of it. Pleased and satisfied, he noted that the outer edge had once again taken on the polish and smooth finish of the surrounding area. Though his fingers detected no other incipient callus or corn, he prudently applied the pumice stone to the soles of both feet, the insteps, and all ten of his toes.

Then, scissors and file in hand, he went about paring and filing his toenails, a most enjoyable pleasure. There, the danger to be warded off was an ingrown toenail. He had an infallible method, the product of his patient observation and his practical imagination: clipping the nail in the shape of a half-moon, leaving at the ends two little intact horns which, thanks to their conformation, would grow out past the flesh without ever imbedding themselves in it. These Saracen toenails, moreover, thanks to their crescent shape, could be cleaned more easily: the point of the file easily penetrated the sort of trench or alveolus between the nail and the flesh where dirt might accumulate, sweat become concentrated, dross find a hiding place. Once he had finished paring, cleaning, and filing his toe-nails, he carefully dug away the cuticles till they were free of those mysterious whitish presences that had crystallized in the remote retreats of his pedal extremities through the work of friction, lack of ventilation, and sweat.

His task ended, he contemplated and massaged his feet with fond satisfaction. He took the parings and filth that he had gathered on a piece of toilet paper, threw it into the bowl, and flushed it down; then he soaped his feet and rinsed them carefully. After drying them, he dusted them with a semi-invisible talcum powder that gave off a slight, virile odor, of heliotrope at dawn.

Invariable ritual procedures remained to be completed: mouth and armpits. Though he concentrated his five senses on them, taking all the time needed to ensure the success of the operation, he had so completely mastered the rite that his attention could be divided and be partially devoted, as well, to a principle of aesthetics, a different one each day of the week, one extracted from that manual, tablet of the law, or commandments drawn up by himself, in secret also, in these nocturnal sessions which, on the pretext of cleanliness, constituted his particular religion and his personal way of bringing about a utopia.

As he laid out on the slab of ocher marble, veined with white, the constituents of the buccal offering— a glassful of water, dental floss, toothpaste, toothbrush—he selected one of the postulates of which he was most certain, a principle which, once formulated, he had never doubted: "Everything bright is ugly, and, first and foremost, brilliant men." He took in a mouthful of water and rinsed his oral cavity vigorously, noting in the mirror how his cheeks puffed out as he rinsed his mouth to rid it of the loosest residual particles, lodged in his gums or superficially suspended between his teeth. There are brilliant cities, brilliant paintings and poems, parties, landscapes, business deals, dissertations, he thought. They should be shunned like weak currencies, however brightly colored the bank notes, or like those tropical drinks for tourists, decorated with fruit slices and little pennants and sweetened with corn syrup.

He was now holding, between the thumb and index finger of each hand, a piece of dental floss twenty centimeters long. He began as always with the upper teeth, from right to left and then from left to right, using his incisors as anchor points. He worked the thread into the narrow interstices and with it raised the edges of the gum, which was where nasty little bread crumbs, shreds of meat, vegetable fibers, bits of fruit skin always lodged. With childish rapture he saw those illegitimate presences emerge, dislodged by the dental floss and his expert acrobatics. He spit them out in the washbasin and saw them slide down the drain and disappear, borne away in the vortex formed by the waterspout from the faucet. Meanwhile, he thought: There are bright heads of hair that crown dim brains or make them become so. The ugliest word in Spanish is brilliantine. As he finished brushing his upper teeth, he again rinsed his mouth and cleaned the length of dental floss in the stream of water from the faucet. Then, with the same vigor and identical professionalism, he began cleaning his lower teeth and molars. There are brilliant conversations, brilliant pieces of music, brilliant illnesses such as allergy to pollen, gout, depressions, and stress. There are, naturally, brilliant brilliant-cut diamonds. He rinsed his mouth out again and threw the piece of dental floss into the wastebasket.

He was now ready to brush his teeth with toothpaste. He did so, brushing downward, slowly, pressing hard so that the bristles—natural ones, never plastic—would penetrate the intimate depths of those bony crevices in search of the residues of food that had survived the sapper's labor of the dental floss. He brushed the lingual surface first, then the buccal. When he rinsed his mouth out for the last time, he felt that agreeable sensation of mint and lemon, so refreshing and youthful, as if all of a sudden, in that cavity framed by gums and palate, someone had turned on an electric fan or the air conditioner and his teeth and molars had ceased to be those hard and insensitive bones and had been imbued with the sensitivity of lips. My teeth are bright, he thought with a twinge of anxiety. Well, that may be the exception that proves the rule. There are, he thought, bright plants, such as the rose. And bright animals such as the Angora cat. All at once he imagined Doña Lucrecia naked, playing with a dozen Angora kittens rubbing against all the curvaceous contours of her lovely body, meowing, and out of fear of experiencing a premature erection, he hastened to wash his armpits. He did so several times a day: in the morning, as he showered, and at noon in the bathroom of the insurance company, before going out for lunch. But it was only now, in the nightly ritual, that he did so conscientiously and at the same time thoroughly enjoying it, neither more nor less than if this were a forbidden pleasure. He first rinsed both armpits with warm water, and his arms as well, rubbing them hard to stimulate the circulation. Then he filled the washbasin with hot water, in which he dissolved a bit of scented soap till he saw the liquid surface begin to foam. He plunged each arm by turn in the warmly welcome temperature and scrubbed his armpits patiently and affectionately, tangling and disentangling the long dark curls of hair in the soapy water. Meanwhile, his mind went on: There are bright, sharp scents, such as that of the rose and camphor. Finally he dried himself and daubed his armpits with a breath of very light cologne suggestive of the smell of skin wet with seawater or that of an ocean breeze that had wafted through hothouses, taking on the heavy scent of flowers.

I am perfect, he thought, looking at himself in the mirror, smelling himself. There was not a whit of vanity in this reflection of his. The object of this laborious care of his body was not to make him better-looking or less ugly, affectations that in one way or another—most often unconsciously—rendered homage to the gregarious ideal that he disdained—wasn't one always "good-looking" to others?—but to make him feel that, in this way, he was somehow halting time's cruel work of undermining, that he was thereby controlling or delaying the fateful deterioration decreed for everything by wicked Nature. The feeling that he was waging this battle did his soul good. Moreover, since he had married, and without Lucrecia's knowledge, he was also fighting his bodily decline in the name of his spouse. Like Amadís in the name of Oriana, he thought. In and on your behalf, my love.

The prospect, once he had turned out the light and left the bathroom, of finding his wife in their bed, awaiting him in a sensual, half-drowsing state, all her turgescences ready and willing to be awakened by his caresses, gave him gooseflesh all over. "You've reached the age of forty and you've never been more beautiful," he murmured, heading for the door. "I love you, Lucrecia."

A second before the bathroom lay in darkness again, he noticed in one of the mirrors on the dressing table that his emotions and wild imaginings had suddenly turned his humanity into a belligerent silhouette, into a profile that had something in common with that wondrous beast of medieval mythologies: the unicorn.

Seven.
Venus,
with Love and Music

She is Venus, the Italian one, the daughter of Jupiter, the sister of Greek Aphrodite. The organ player gives her music lessons. My name is Love. Tiny, delicate, rosy, winged, I am a thousand years old and chaste as a dragonfly. The stag, the royal peacock, and the fallow deer that can be seen through the window are as alive as the pair of lovers strolling arm in arm in the shade of the promenade lined with poplars. The satyr of the fountain, however, into whose head crystalline water flows from an alabaster basin, is not alive: it is a piece of Tuscan marble modeled by a clever artist come from the South of France.

We three are alive, too, and as vivacious as the little stream that sings its way down the mountainside between the rocks or the chatter of the parrots that a trader from Africa sold to Don Rigoberto, our master. (The captive animals are now languishing in a cage in the garden.) Twilight has fallen and soon it will be night. When it comes with its lead-gray tatters, the organ will fall silent and the music teacher and I must leave so that the lord and master of everything to be seen here may enter this room to possess his lady. At that time, by our will and through our work well done, Venus will be ready to receive him and entertain him as his rank and fortune merit. That is to say, with the fire of a volcano, the sensuality of a serpent, and the hauteur of a pampered Angora cat.

The young music teacher and I are not here to enjoy ourselves but to work, though all work done wholeheartedly and well turns, it is true, into pleasure. Our task consists of kindling the lady's bodily joy, poking up the ashes of each one of her five senses till they burst into flame, and peopling her fair-haired head with filthy fantasies. That is how Don Rigoberto likes to have us hand her over to him: ardent and avid, all her moral and religious scruples in abeyance and her mind and body filled to overflowing with appetites. It is an agreeable task, though not an easy one; it requires patience, cunning, and skill in the art of attuning the fury of instinct to the mind's subtlety and the heart's tender affections.

The repetitive, churchly strains of the organ create an auspicious atmosphere. It is generally thought that the organ, so closely associated with the Mass

Titian, *Venus with Cupid and Music*,
oil on canvas, The Prado, Madrid

and the religious hymn, desensualizes and even disincarnates the humble mortal bathed in its waves. A gross error; in truth, organ music, with its obsessive languor and its soft purr, merely disconnects the Christian from the world and from contingency, isolating his mind so that it may turn toward something exclusive and different: God and salvation, quite true, in countless cases; but also, in many others, sin, perdition, lust, and other harsh municipal synonyms for what is expressed by that limpid word: pleasure.

The sound of the organ calms the lady and quiets her mind: a flaccid immobility not unlike ecstasy steals over her and she then half closes her eyes so as to concentrate more intently on the melody which, as it invades her, removes from her mind the preoccupations and the petty concerns of the day and drains it of everything that is not audition, pure sensation. That is how it begins. The teacher plays with an agile, self-assured, unhurried touch, in a soft, melting crescendo, choosing ambiguous compositions that discreetly transport us to austere retreats under the monastic rule of Saint Bernard, to street processions that are suddenly transformed into a pagan carnival, and thence, without transition, to the Gregorian chant of an abbey or the sung Mass of a cathedral attended by a profusion of cardinals, and finally to a promiscuous masked ball in a mansion on the outskirts of the city. Wine flows in abundance and there are suspicious movements in the leafy bowers of the garden. A beautiful maiden, sitting in the lap of a lustful, potbellied old gaffer, suddenly removes her mask. And who does she turn out to be? One of the stable boys! Or the androgynous village idiot with a man's cock and a woman's tits! My lady sees this series of images because I describe them to her in her ear, in a soft, perverse voice, in time to the music. My vast knowledge translates the notes of the organ that is my accomplice into provocative shapes, colors, figures, actions. That is what I am doing now, more or less perched on her back, my smooth little face jutting out over her shoulder like a sharp-pointed prod: whispering naughty stories to her. Fictions that distract her and make her smile, fictions that shock and excite her.

The teacher cannot leave off playing the organ for a single moment: his life depends on it. Don Rigoberto has warned him: "If those bellows stop working for one moment, I will know that you have yielded to the temptation to touch. I shall then plunge this dagger into your heart and throw your dead body to the dogs. We shall now find out which is stronger in you, young man: desire for my fair spouse or attachment to your life." Attachment to his life, naturally.

But as the pipes throb, he has the right to look. It is a privilege that honors and exalts him, that makes him feel himself to be a monarch or a god. He takes advantage of it with delicious pleasure. His glances, moreover, make my task easier and complement it, since the lady, noting the fervor and the homage rendered her by the eyes of that beardless countenance and intuiting the feverish cravings that her voluptuous white contours arouse in that sensitive adolescent, cannot but feel deeply touched and in the grip of concupiscent humors.

Above all, when the organ player looks at her there where his gaze is fixed. What is the young musician finding, or what is he asking in that intimate Venusian retreat? What are his virgin pupils endeavoring to penetrate? What is so powerfully magnetizing him in that triangle of transparent skin, traversed in circular paths by little blue veins like rivulets, cast in shadow by the depilated thicket of her pubis? I could not say; nor, I believe, could he. But there is something there that attracts his eyes in the late afternoon each day, with the imperiousness of a stroke of fate or the magic of a witch's spell. Something like the divination that, at the foot of the sunlit mound of Venus, in the tender cleft protected by the rounded columns of the lady's thighs, resilient, red, moist with the dew of her privateness, pours forth the fountain of life and pleasure. In just a little while now, our lord and master Don Rigoberto will bend down to drink ambrosia from it. The organ player knows that this draft will forever be forbidden him, since he will soon be entering the Dominican monastery. He is a pious lad who from the tender years of his childhood felt the call of God and whom nothing or no one will keep from the priesthood. Even though, as he has confessed to me, these twilight parties make him break into an icy sweat and people his dreams with demons tricked out in a woman's tits and buttocks, they have not undermined his religious vocation. On the contrary: they have convinced him of the necessity, in order to save his soul and help others save theirs, of renouncing the pomp and the carnal pleasures of this world. Perhaps he casts his eyes so pertinaciously upon the curly garden of his mistress only to prove to himself and to show God that he is capable of resisting temptations, even the most Luciferian of them: the imperishable body of our lady.

Neither she nor I have these moral dilemmas and problems of conscience. I because I am a little pagan god, and nonexistent besides, nothing more nor less than a fancy of the human imagination, and she because she is an obedient wife who reluctantly goes along with these soirees that are a prelude to the conjugal night, out of respect for her husband, who programs them down to the last detail. She is, then, a lady who bows to the will of her master, as a Christian wife should, so that, if these sensual love feasts are sinful, it is to be supposed that they will blacken only the soul of the person who, for personal pleasure, conceives them and orders them.

My lady's delicate and painstakingly constructed coiffure, with its curls, waves, flirtatious loose locks, rises and falls, and its baroque pearl adornments, is also a spectacle orchestrated by Don Rigoberto. He gave precise instructions to the hairdressers and holds daily inspection, like a military officer reviewing his troops, of the array of jewels in my lady's dowry so as to choose those that will gleam that night in her hair, circle her throat, dangle from her translucent ears, and imprison her fingers and wrists. "You are not you but my fantasy," she says he whispers to her when he makes love to her. "You will not be Lucrecia today but Venus, and today you will change from a Peruvian woman into an Italian one and from a creature of this earth into a goddess and a symbol."

Perhaps that is how she is, in Don Rigoberto's elaborate imaginings. But she is nonetheless real, concrete, as alive as a rose not plucked from the branch, or a little songbird. Is she not a beautiful woman? Yes, wondrously beautiful. Above all, at this instant, when her instincts have begun to awaken, revived by the studied alchemy of the organ's prolonged notes, the tremulous glances of the musician, and the ardent corruptions that I distill into her ear. My left hand feels, there above her breast, how her skin has little by little grown tense and hot. Her blood is beginning to boil. This is the moment when she is at the full, or (to put it in scholarly terms) has reached plenitude, what philosophers term the absolute and alchemists transubstantiation.

The word that best sums up her body is: tumid.

Roused by my salacious fictions, everything about her becomes curve and prominence, sinuous elevation, tempered softness. That is the consistency that the connoisseur should prefer in his partner at the hour of love: tender abundance that appears to be just about to overflow yet remains firm, supple, resilient as ripe fruit and freshly kneaded dough, that soft texture Italians call *morbidezza*, a word that sounds lustful even when applied to bread.

Now that she is already on fire inside, her little head phosphorescing with lubricious images, I shall scale her back and roll about on the satiny geography of her body, tickling her in the proper zones with my wings, and gambol about like a happy little puppy on the warm pillow of her belly. These affected gestures of mine make her laugh, and they kindle her body till it becomes an incandescent coal. My memory is already hearing her laugh that will be forthcoming, a laugh that drowns out the moans of the organ and makes the lips of the young music teacher drool. When she laughs, her nipples grow hard and erect, as though an invisible mouth were sucking them, and the muscles of her stomach ripple beneath the smooth skin with the scent of vanilla that suggests the rich treasure of warmths and moistures of her private parts. At that moment my turned-up nose can catch the faint odor of her secret juices, like a whiff of overripe cheese. The aroma of this amorous suppuration drives Don Rigoberto mad, and he—as she has told me—kneeling as if in prayer, absorbs it and impregnates himself with it to the point of blissful, intoxicated rapture. It is, he maintains, a more powerful aphrodisiac than all the elixirs, compounded of the nastiest substances, hawked to lovers by the sorcerers and procuresses of this city. "As long as that is how you smell, I will be your slave," she says that he says to her, with the loose tongue of those drunk on love.

The door will soon open and we will hear Don Rigoberto's soft footfalls on the carpet. We will soon see him appear at this bedside to ascertain whether the two of us, the music teacher and I, have been capable of bringing base reality closer to his tinseled fantasies. Hearing the lady's laughter, seeing her, breathing in the odor of her, he will take it that something more or less like that has happened. He will then make an almost imperceptible gesture of approval, which for us will be an order to take our leave.

The organ will fall silent; with a deep bow, the music teacher will make his exit by way of the orangery, and I will leap through the window and take off on my flying trapeze into the fragrant dark of the open sky.

The two of them, and the echo of their tender love bout, will remain behind in the boudoir.

Eight.
The Salt of His Tears

Justiniana's eyes were as big as saucers and she was gesticulating wildly. Her hands looked like the vanes of a windmill.

"Little Alfonso says he's going to kill himself! Because you don't love him anymore, he says!" she exclaimed, blinking in terror. "He's writing a farewell letter, señora."

"Is this another one of those wild notions that . . ." Doña Lucrecia stammered, looking at her in the mirror of the dressing table. "More twittering from that birdbrain of yours?"

But the maidservant's face was dead serious and Doña Lucrecia, who was plucking her eyebrows, dropped the tweezers on the floor, and without further questions headed off down the stairs at a run, followed by Justiniana. The boy's bedroom door was locked. His stepmother knocked: "Alfonso, Alfonsito!" There was no answer and not a sound could be heard inside.

"Foncho! Fonchito!" Doña Lucrecia called out insistently, knocking on the door once more. Her back felt ice-cold. "Open the door! Are you all right? Why don't you answer me, Alfonso!"

The key turned with a creak in the lock, but the door did not open. Doña Lucrecia drew a deep breath. The ground beneath her feet was solid again, the world was righting itself after a dizzying slide into chaos.

"Leave me alone with him," she ordered Justiniana.

She entered the room, closing the door behind her. She did her best to repress the indignation that was gradually getting the better of her, now that the scare she had had was over.

Alfonso, still dressed in his school uniform, was sitting at his desk, his head bent. He raised it and looked at her, not moving, sad-faced, more beautiful than ever. Though daylight was still coming in through the window, his study lamp was turned on and in the golden circle falling on the green desk blotter Doña Lucrecia spied a half-finished letter, the ink still glistening, an uncapped pen lying alongside his little hand with inkstained fingers.

She crossed the room slowly and halted beside him. "What are you doing?" she murmured.

Her voice and her hands were trembling, her breast heaving.

"Writing a letter," the boy replied, in a firm voice. "To you."

"To me?" She smiled, making an effort to appear pleased. "May I read it?"

Alfonso put his hand over the paper. His hair was touseled, his face grave. "Not yet." There was an adult determination in his eyes and his tone of voice was defiant. "It's a farewell letter."

"A farewell letter? Does that mean, then, that you're going off somewhere, Fonchito?"

"I'm going to kill myself," Doña Lucrecia heard him say, his gaze riveted on her, not moving a muscle. Yet, after a few seconds, his composure suddenly left him and his eyes brimmed with tears. "Because you don't love me anymore, stepmother."

Hearing herself told that in this way, half in grief and half in anger, the boy's little face puckering into a pout that he tried in vain to control, in the words of a dejected lover which sounded so incongruous coming from this beardless figure in knee pants, left Doña Lucrecia dumbfounded. She stood there openmouthed, not knowing what to say in reply.

"What do you mean by such foolishness, Fonchito?" she finally murmured, only halfway pulling herself together. "I don't love you, you say? But, darling, how can that be, if you're like my own son. You're the one I . . ."

She fell silent, because Alfonso, flinging himself upon her and putting his arms around her waist, burst into tears. Pressing his face against Doña Lucrecia's belly, he sobbed and sobbed, his little body shaken with sighs, his panting like a famished puppy's. Yes, at this moment, no doubt about it, he was a child, given the despair with which he wept and the shamelessness with which he manifested his suffering. Fighting not to allow herself to be overcome by the emotion that gripped her throat and filled her eyes with tears, Doña Lucrecia stroked his hair. Confused, a prey to contradictory feelings, she listened to him unburden himself, in a rush of stammered complaints.

"You haven't spoken to me for days now. I ask you something and you turn away. You don't let me kiss you good night or good morning, and when I come back from school you look at me as if it annoyed you to see me come home. Why, stepmother? What have I done?"

Doña Lucrecia contradicted him and kissed his hair. No, Fonchito, none of that is true. You are hurt much too easily, sweetie! And, searching for the kindest way to put it, she tried to explain. Of course she loved him! A whole lot, darling! She worried about him all the time and thought about him every minute when he was at school or playing soccer with his friends. It was just that it wasn't good for him to be so attached to her, to love his stepmother to distraction like that. It could do him harm, silly boy, if he allowed himself to be so impulsive, to have such strong feelings. It would be better for him emotionally if he didn't depend on someone like her so much, someone so much older than he. His affection, his interests ought to be shared with other people, be directed above all toward boys his own age, his friends at school, his cousins. He would grow up sooner that way, with a personality of his own, be the upright young man that she and Don Rigoberto would have every reason to be so proud of later.

But as Doña Lucrecia spoke, something in her heart belied what she was saying. She was certain, moreover, that the boy wasn't listening to her. Perhaps he didn't even hear her. I don't believe a single word of what I'm telling him, she thought. Now that his sobs had ceased, though every so often he heaved a deep sigh, Alfonsito's attention appeared to be riveted on his stepmother's hands. He had seized them and was kissing them lingeringly, timidly, with fervent devotion. Then, as he rubbed them against his satiny cheek, Doña Lucrecia heard him murmur in a very soft voice, as though he were addressing only the slender fingers that he was squeezing so hard: "I love you a lot, stepmother. A whole lot . . . Don't ever treat me again the way you have lately, because I'll kill myself. I swear to you I'll kill myself."

And then it was as though a dam had suddenly burst within her and a flood descended upon her prudence and her reason, submerging them, pulverizing ancestral principles she had never doubted, and even her instinct for self-preservation. She squatted down, bent one knee so as to be at the same height as the seated boy, and embraced and caressed him, free of all constraint, a stranger to herself, and as though caught in the eye of a storm.

"Never again," she repeated, haltingly, for emotion scarcely permitted her to get the words out. "I promise you I'll never treat you that way again. The coldness of these recent days was a pretense, lambikins. How stupid I've been: I wanted to do you a kindness, and I've made you suffer. Forgive me, love . . ."

And at the same time she kissed him on his touseled hair, on his forehead, on his cheeks, tasting on her lips the salt of his tears. When the boy's mouth sought hers, she did not refuse it to him. Half closing her eyes, she let herself be kissed and returned the kiss. After a moment, emboldened, the boy's lips pressed down hard on hers and then she opened hers and allowed a nervous little viper, clumsy and frightened at first, and then rash, to visit her mouth and explore it, gliding across her gums and her teeth from one side to the other. Nor did she push away the hand she suddenly felt on one of her breasts. It rested there for a moment, perfectly still, as though summoning strength, and then, forming a hollow, caressed it with a delicate, respectful squeeze. Even though, in the depths of her mind, a voice urged her to get to her feet and leave, Doña Lucrecia did not move. Instead, she hugged the boy to her and, with no inhibitions, went on kissing him with an impetuousness and a wantonness that mounted step by step with her desire. Till the moment when, as in dreams, she heard a car brake to a stop and, shortly thereafter, her husband's voice calling to her.

She leapt to her feet in terror; her panic communicated itself to the boy, whose eyes were suddenly filled with fear. She saw Alfonso's clothes in disarray, the traces of lipstick on his mouth. "Go wash your face," she hurriedly ordered him, pointing, and the boy nodded and ran to the bathroom.

She came out of the bedroom in a daze and practically staggered across the little sitting room overlooking the garden. She went into the guest bathroom and locked herself in. Her legs were about to give way, as though she had been running. Looking at herself in the mirror, she was seized with a fit of hysterical laughter that she stifled by clapping her hand over her mouth. "You stupid fool, you madwoman," she berated herself as she wet her face with cold water. Then she sat down on the bidet and let the jet run for a long time. She carefully tidied herself and straightened her clothes and composed her features and stayed there in the bathroom till she felt altogether calm again, in complete control of her facial expression and her gestures. When she came out to greet her husband, she was as fresh and smiling as though nothing out of the ordinary had happened to her. Nonetheless, though Don Rigoberto found her as affectionate and solicitous as always, leaning over backward to pamper and indulge him, and listening, with the same interest as usual, to his stories of how the day had gone, there was a hidden malaise in Doña Lucrecia that did not leave her for an instant, an edginess that, every so often, made her shiver and her stomach feel hollow.

The youngster had dinner with them. He was polite and nicely behaved, his usual self. He greeted his father's jokes with bubbling laughter and even asked him to tell some more, "off-color ones, Papa, the kind that are a tiny bit dirty." When her eyes met his, Doña Lucrecia was surprised not to find in that clear, pale blue gaze the least shadow of a cloud, the slightest gleam of impishness or connivance.

Hours later, in the privacy of their darkened bedroom, Don Rigoberto whispered once again that he loved her and, covering her with kisses, thanked her for his days and nights, the immense bliss that filled his life because of her. "Since we've been married, I've been learning how to live, Lucrecia," she heard him tell her excitedly. "Had it not been for you, I would have died without ever knowing that such wisdom existed and without even suspecting what pleasure really meant." As she listened to him, she was moved and happy, but even now she couldn't stop thinking about the youngster. Nonetheless, that intruding proximity, that curious angelical presence did not detract from her pleasure, but, on the contrary, enhanced it with a feverish, disturbing piquancy.

"Aren't you going to ask me who I am?" Don Rigoberto finally murmured.

"Who, who, my love?" she asked with the requisite impatience, spurring him on.

"Well, a monster," she heard him say, already far away, unreachable, in his flight of fancy.

Nine.
Profile of
a Human Being

My left ear was bitten off in a fight with another
human being, as I remember. But I hear the sounds
of the world clearly through the thin slit that remains. I also see things, though only obliquely and
with difficulty. Because, even though not apparent
at first glance, this bluish protuberance, to the left
of my mouth, is an eye. That it is there, in working
order, apprehending forms and colors, is a marvel
wrought by medical science, a testimonial to the
extraordinary progress so characteristic of our time.
I ought by all odds to be doomed to perpetual darkness, since all the survivors of the great fire—I do
not recall whether it was caused by a bombardment
or a coup d'état—lost both their sight and their hair,
because of the oxides. I had the good fortune to lose
only one eye; the other one was saved by the ophthal-
mologists after sixteen operations. It has no eyelid

and frequently oozes tears, but it allows me to distract myself watching television and, above all, to detect in a flash the appearance of the enemy.

The glass cube I live in is my home. I can see through the walls of it, but no one can see me from the outside: a very handy system for ensuring the safety of the home, in this era of terrible traps. The glass panes of my dwelling are, of course, bulletproof, germproof, radiationproof, and soundproof. They are continually perfumed with the distinctive odor of armpits and musk, which to me—and only to me, I know—is delightful.

I have a very highly developed sense of smell and it is by way of my nose that I experience the greatest pleasure and the greatest pain. Ought I to call this gigantic membranous organ that registers all scents, even the most subtle, a nose? I am referring to the grayish shape, covered with white crusts, that begins at my mouth and extends, increasing in size, down to my bull neck. No, it is not a goiter or an acromegalic Adam's apple. It is my nose. I know that it is neither beautiful nor useful, since its excessive sensibility makes it an indescribable torment when a rat is rotting in the vicinity or fetid materials pass through the drainpipes that run through my home. Nonetheless, I revere it and sometimes think that my nose is the seat of my soul.

I have no arms or legs, but my four stumps are nicely healed over and well toughened, so that I can move about easily along the ground and can even

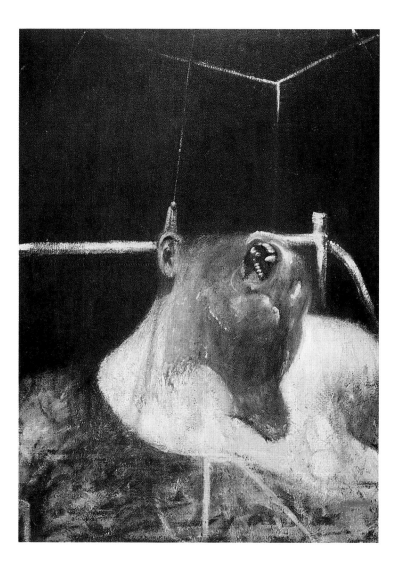

Francis Bacon, *Head I* (1948),
oil and tempera on hardboard,
collection of Richard S. Zeisler, New York

run if need be. My enemies have never been able to catch me in any of their roundups thus far. How did I lose my hands and feet? An accident at work, perhaps; or maybe some medicine my mother took so as to have an easy pregnancy (science doesn't come up with the right answer in all cases, unfortunately).

My sex organ is intact. I can make love, on condition that the young fellow or the female acting as my *partenaire* allows me to position myself in such a way that my boils don't rub against his or her body, for if they burst they leak stinking pus and I suffer terrible pain. I like to fornicate, and I would say that, in a certain sense, I am a voluptuary. I often have fiascoes or experience a humiliating premature ejaculation, it is true. But, other times, I have prolonged and repeated orgasms that give me the sensation of being as ethereal and radiant as the Archangel Gabriel. The repulsion I inspire in my lovers turns into attraction, and even into delirium, once they overcome—thanks almost always to alcohol or drugs—their initial prejudices and agree to do amorous battle with me on a bed. Women even come to love me, in fact, and youngsters become addicted to my ugliness. In the depths of her soul, Beauty was always fascinated by the Beast, as so many fantastic tales and mythologies recount, and it is only in rare cases that the heart of a good-looking youth does not harbor something perverse. No one has ever regretted being my lover. Males and females alike thank me for having given them advanced instruction in the fine art of combining desire and the horrible so as to give pleasure. They learned from me that everything is and can be erogenous and that, associated with love, the basest organic functions, including those of the lower abdomen, become spiritualized and ennobled. The dance of gerunds they perform with me—belching, urinating, defecating—lingers with them afterward like a memory of times gone by, that descent into filth (something that tempts all of them yet few dare to undertake) made in my company.

My greatest source of pride is my mouth. It is not true that it is open wide because I am forever howling in despair. I keep it wide open like that to show off my sharp white teeth. Is there anyone who wouldn't envy them? I'm missing only two or three of them. The rest are still strong and carnivorous. If necessary, they crush stones. But they prefer to feed on the breasts and hindquarters of calves, to sink into the little tits and thighs of hens and capons or the throats of little birds. Eating flesh is a prerogative of the gods.

I am not a miserable wretch, nor do I want people to pity me. I am what I am and that's enough for me. Knowing that others are worse off is a great consolation, of course. It is possible that God exists, but at this point in history, with everything that has happened to us, does it matter? That the world might have been better than it is? Yes, perhaps, but what's the use of mulling over a question like that? I've survived and, despite appearances, I am part of the human race.

Take a good look at me, my love. Recognize me, and recognize yourself.

Ten.

Tuberous and Sensual

"Once upon a time, there was a man attached to a nose," Don Rigoberto recited, beginning the Thursday ceremony with a poetic invocation. And he remembered José María Eguren, the slender nephelibate poet who, regarding the Spanish word *nariz* as being phonetically vulgar, gallicized it and called it *nez* in his poems.

Was his nose extremely ugly? It depended on the looking glass in which it was contemplated. It was round and hooked, without inferiority complexes, curious about the world, very sensitive, tuberous, and ornamental. Despite Don Rigoberto's attentions and precautions, its appearance was marred from time to time by a rash of blackheads, but this week, to judge from what the mirror told him, not one had shown up to be squeezed, pressed out, and immediately disinfected with peroxide. Through an inexplicable cutaneous caprice, a good part of it, the lower end in particular, there where it curved and opened out to form two windows, had a reddish tinge to it, that aged-burgundy color that so often is a telltale sign of a souse. But Don Rigoberto drank in as great moderation as he ate, so that those red splotches had no other possible cause, in his opinion, than the vagaries and caprices of Dame Nature. Unless—the face of Doña Lucrecia's husband broke into a smile that stretched from ear to ear—his big sensitive schnoz had taken on a permanent blush at the memory of the libidinous bodily needs he sniffed in the conjugal bed. Don Rigoberto noted that the two orifices of his respiratory organ immediately distended, anticipating those seminal breezes—emulsifying fragrances, he thought—that in a short while, entering therein, would impregnate him to the very marrow. He felt especially favored and grateful. To work, then, for there was a time and a place for everything: this is not yet the right moment for breathing exercises, you rascal.

Using his handkerchief, he blew his nose, hard, first one side and then the other, and with his index finger he blocked the opposite nostril each time, till he was certain that his nose was free of mucosities and watery secretions. Then, holding in his left hand the philatelist's loupe that he was in the habit of using to explore the postcards and erotic etchings in his collection and as an aid in his meticulous cleansing ritual, and with his little nail scissors in his right, he proceeded to rid his nostrils of those tiny anti-aesthetic hairs whose small black heads were already beginning to be visible from the outside, despite their having been decapitated just seven days before. The task called for the concentration of an Oriental miniaturist to carry it out successfully without cutting himself. It brought Don Rigoberto a soothing spiritual serenity, little short of the state of "emptiness and fullness" described by mystics.

His iron will to control the unpleasant arbitrary acts of his body, forcing it to exist within certain aesthetic rules, never going beyond limits fixed by his sovereign taste—and, to a certain extent, Lucrecia's—thanks to techniques of extirpation, trimming, expulsion, irrigation, friction, tonsure, polishing, et cetera, which he had finally mastered, as an excellent workman masters his craft, isolated him from the rest of humanity and produced in him that miraculous sensation—which would reach its apogee when he joined his wife in the darkness of the bedroom—of having escaped from time. More than a sensation: a physical certainty. All his cells were freed at that instant—snip snip went the silvery blades of the little scissors and snip snip the little clipped hairs drifted slowly, weightlessly, through the air, snip snip from his nostrils to the whirlpool in the washbasin, snip snip—reprieved, absolved of the deterioration of occurring, of the nightmare of persisting in being. That was the magic virtue of the rite, and primitive man had discovered it at the dawn of history: transforming one, for certain eternal instants, into sheer being-present. He had rediscovered that wisdom all by himself, on his own and at his own risk. He thought: The way of withdrawing momentarily from the base decadence and the civil servitudes of the social order, the abject conventions of the herd, in order to attain, for one brief parenthesis per day, a sovereign nature. He thought: This is a foretaste of immortality. The word did not strike him as excessive. At this instant he felt himself to be—snip snip snip snip—incorruptible, and, soon now, in the arms and between the legs of his spouse, he would feel himself to be a monarch. He thought: A god.

The bathroom was his temple; the washbasin, the sacrificial altar; he was the high priest and was celebrating the Mass that each night purified him and redeemed him from life. "In a moment I shall be worthy of Lucrecia and be with her," he said to himself. Thus absorbed in contemplation, he addressed his strong nose in warm tones: "I say unto you that very soon you and I shall be in Paradise, my good thief." Catching the scent of the future, his two orifices opened greedily. But instead of the intimate, prehensile aromas of the lady of the house, they took in the aseptic odor of soapy water which Don Rigoberto, by means of complicated manual aspersions and equine tossings of his head, was now applying, as a final touch, to the freshly clipped interior of his nostrils.

The delicate phase of the nasal rite being ended, his mind could now abandon itself once again to the play of fantasy, and all of a sudden, it associated the imminent nuptial bed, where Lucrecia lay awaiting him, with the unpronounceable name of the Dutch historian and essayist Johan Huizinga, one of whose essays had touched the depths of his heart, persuading him that it had been written for him, for her, for the two of them. Giving the soul of his nose one last rinse with pure water through a medicine dropper, Don Rigoberto asked himself: "Isn't our bed the magic space that *Homo ludens* speaks of?" Yes, by antonomasia. According to the Dutch writer, culture, civilization, war, sports, law, religion had sprung from that territory bound by rules, as arborescences and luxuriant leafy growths, some of them felicitous, others perverse, of the irresistible human propensity for game playing. An amusing theory, doubtless; a subtle one as well, but surely false. The decorous humanist, however, had refrained from pursuing his flash of genius to the farthest depths, applying it to the domain that confirmed his intuition, where nearly everything became clear thanks to the light it shed.

"A magic space, a feminine realm, the grove of the senses": he searched for metaphors for the little country that Lucrecia was inhabiting at this moment. "My kingdom is a bed," he decreed, rinsing his hands now, drying them. The vast triple-width mattress allowed the couple to move comfortably in any direction, to stretch out, and roll over and over in free and joyous embrace without risk of falling to the floor. It was soft but resilient, with firm springs, and so perfectly level that any of their members could glide over it without encountering the slightest roughness or obstacle that would conspire against any given gymnastic exercise, pose, daring overture, or clever sculptural parody during their love games. "The Abbey of Incontinence," Don Rigoberto ventured, in a moment of inspiration. "A garden-plot mattress, where my wife's flowers open and yield their secret essences to this privileged mortal."

He noted in the mirror that his nostrils had begun to throb like two famished little gullets. "Let me get a deep breath of you, my love." He would sniff her and breathe her in from head to foot, with meticulous care and perseverance, lingering long at certain areas with their own special odor, and hurrying past others, vapid and uninteresting: he would subject her to intense nasal scrutiny and make love to her, hearing her demur every so often amid stifled giggles. "Oh, no, my love, you're tickling me." Don Rigoberto felt a bit light-headed with impatience. But he took his time: a wait in store brings hope of even more; one prepares to take one's pleasure with greater discernment and discrimination.

He had just arrived at the final stages of the ceremony when, from the garden, filtering through the joints of the windowpanes, the penetrating perfume of honeysuckle reached his nostrils. He closed his eyes and inhaled. The scent of that rambling climber was a treacherous one. It stayed shut up tight for days without giving forth its green aroma, as though hoarding it and concentrating it, and then, all of a sudden, at certain mysterious moments of the day or night, owing to the humidity in the air, or the movements of the moon and stars, or certain circumspect cataclysms down below, there in the bosom of the earth in which it was rooted, it discharged upon the world that disturbing, bittersweet breath that called to mind swarthy-skinned women with long wavy hair, and dances that offered, in their wanton whirl of skirts, a glimpse of satiny thighs, dark buttocks, delicate ankles, and, swift will-o'-the-wisp, the tangle of a luxuriant pubis.

Yes, now—Don Rigoberto's eyes were closed and it was as if all his energy had fled his body and taken refuge in his reproductive and nasal organs—his nostrils were breathing in Doña Lucrecia's honeysuckle. And as the warm, heavy perfume, with hints of musk, incense, sauerkraut, anise, pickled herring, violets opening, moist secretions of a virgin maiden, mounted to his brain like an emanation from the vegetable kingdom or a sulfurous lava, bringing on an eruption of desire, his nose, transformed into a sensitive plant, could also catch the scent now of that beloved grove, the viscous friction of that slit of bright lips, the tickle of that moist fleece whose fine silky hairs agitated his nasal orifices, further enhancing the effect of a vaporous narcotic being offered him by the body of his beloved.

Making an intense intellectual effort—to recite aloud the Pythagorean theorem—Don Rigoberto halted halfway in its course the erection that was beginning to bare its amorous little head, and splashing it with handfuls of cold water, he calmed it down and returned it, shy and shrunken, to its discreet foreskin cocoon. He fondly contemplated the soft cylinder which, serene now, elastic, swinging back and forth like the clapper of a bell, prolonged his lower belly. He told himself once again that it was a great stroke of luck that it had not occurred to his parents to have him circumcised: his prepuce was a diligent producer of pleasing sensations, and he was certain that, had he been deprived of this translucent membrane, his nights of love would have been the poorer, a privation as grave as if an evil spell had destroyed his sense of smell.

And he suddenly remembered those bold eccentrics for whom breathing in peculiar odors, regarded as repellent by the ordinary individual, was a vital necessity, to precisely the same degree as eating and drinking. He tried to picture in his mind the poet Friedrich von Schiller avidly burying his sensitive nostrils in the rotten apples that stimulated him and predisposed him to creation and love, precisely as little erotic figures did Don Rigoberto. And then he allowed his imagination to dwell upon the unsettling private recipe of that elegant historian of the French Revolution, François Michelet—one of whose vagaries was to keep an observant eye on his beloved Athéné as she menstruated; on finding himself overcome with fatigue and thoroughly discouraged, he was in the habit of abandoning the manuscripts, parchments, and filing cabinets of his study and silently stealing, like a thief, into the water closet of their home. Don Rigoberto conjured up a mental image of him: in a swallowtail coat, pumps, and a frilled shirt perhaps, kneeling reverently before the toilet bowl, absorbing with infantile delight the fetid miasmas which, once they reached the labyrinthine folds of his romantic brain, restored his enthusiasms and his energy, refreshed his mind and his body, revived his intellectual drive and his generous ideals. What a normal man I am, compared to those queer birds, he thought. But he did not feel disheartened or inferior. The bliss he had found in his solitary hygienic practices and, above all, in the love of his wife appeared to him to be sufficient compensation for his normalcy. Having this, what need was there to be rich, famous, eccentric, a genius? The modest obscurity that his life represented in the eyes of others, that routine existence as the general manager of an insurance company, concealed something which, he was sure, few of his fellows enjoyed or even suspected existed: possible happiness. Transitory and secret, yes, minimal even, but certain, palpable, nightly, alive. He was now feeling it all about him, surrounding him like an aureole, and in a few minutes he would be that happiness, and it would also be his wife, together with him and with it, united in that profound trinity of two who, thanks to pleasure, were one, or rather, three. Had he perhaps resolved the mystery of the Trinity? He smiled: it's not that big a deal, you rascal. Just a pinch of wisdom to use as a momentary antidote to the frustrations and annoyances that seasoned existence. He thought: Fantasy gnaws life away, thank God.

As he stepped through the door of the bedroom, he gave a tremulous sigh.

Eleven.
After Dinner

"I'm going to tell you something you don't know, stepmother," Alfonso exclaimed, with a vibrant little gleam in his eye. "You're in the painting in the living room."

His face was excited and playful, and he was hoping, with an impish half smile, that she would guess what was behind the hint he had just given her.

He's a child again, Doña Lucrecia thought from inside the warm cocoon of languor in which she found herself, halfway between sleep and waking. Only a moment before, he had been a youth without scruples, of unerring instinct, riding her like an expert horseman. And now he was a happy child once more, delighting in propounding riddles to his adoptive mother. He was squatting on his heels, naked, at the foot of the bed, and she was unable to resist the temptation to reach out her hand and place it on that fair-skinned thigh, the color of honey, covered with a barely visible down glistening with sweat. That's what Greek gods must have looked like, she thought. The little cupids in paintings, the pages who were the attendants of princesses, the little genies of *The Thousand and One Nights*, the *spintria* of Suetonius' book. She sank her fingers into that young, resilient flesh and thought, with a voluptuous shiver: You're as happy as a queen, Lucrecia.

"But that's a Szyszlo in the living room," she murmured halfheartedly. "An abstract painting, sweetie."

Alfonsito let out a hearty laugh.

"Well, it's you," he declared. And suddenly he blushed to the ears, as though warmed by a strong solar current. "I first noticed this morning. But I won't tell you how I discovered it, even if you kill me."

He was overcome by another fit of giggles and let himself fall face down on the bed. He remained in that position for some time, his face buried in the pillow, quaking with laughter. "Whatever notion can you have gotten into that crazy little head of yours now?" Doña Lucrecia murmured, ruffling his hair, as fine as sand or rice powder. "Some bad thought, you bandit, since you're blushing like anything."

They had spent the night together for the first time, taking advantage of one of those lightning-quick business trips to the provinces that Don Rigoberto often took. The day before, Doña Lucrecia had given all the servants the night off, so that the two of them were alone in the house. That evening, after having dinner together and watching television as they waited for Justiniana and the cook to leave, they went upstairs to the bedroom and made love before going to sleep. And made love again when they woke up, just a short while later, with the first morning light. Behind the chocolate-colored window blinds, the day soon grew brighter and brighter. There were already the sounds of people and cars in the street. The servants would soon be arriving. They had a hearty breakfast, with fruit juice and scrambled eggs. At noon, she and Alfonsito would go to the airport to pick up her husband. She had never said anything about it to Alfonsito, but they both knew that Don Rigoberto was always delighted to see them there waving to him as he got off the plane, and whenever they could, they gave him that pleasure.

"So I know now what's meant by an abstract painting," the youngster reflected, without raising his head from the pillow. "A dirty picture! I had no idea."

Doña Lucrecia leaned over toward him. She rested her cheek on his smooth back, without a drop of oil on it, gleaming as though with hoarfrost, revealing just the barest hint of his spinal column, like a miniature cordillera. She closed her eyes and seemed to hear the slow pulse of precocious blood beneath the supple skin. It's life beating, life living, she thought in amazement.

Since making love with the boy for the first time, she had lost her scruples and that feeling of guilt that had so troubled her before. It had happened on the day following the episode of the letter and his threats to kill himself. It had been something so unexpected that when Doña Lucrecia remembered it, it seemed impossible to her, something not experienced in real life but dreamed of or read about. Don Rigoberto had just shut himself up in the bathroom for his nightly personal hygiene ceremony and she, in a negligee and a nightgown, had gone downstairs to say good night to Alfonsito, as she had promised. The boy leapt out of bed to greet her. Clinging to her neck, he sought her lips and timidly caressed her breasts, as the two of them heard, above their heads, like background music, Don Rigoberto humming an operetta—out of tune, with the water running into the washbasin serving as counterpoint. And, all of a sudden, Doña Lucrecia felt an aggressive, virile presence against her body. It had been more powerful than her sense of danger, an uncontrollable ecstasy. She allowed herself to fall back on the bed as she drew the youngster to her, not at all abruptly, as though fearful of crushing him to bits. Opening her negligee and drawing aside her nightdress, she positioned him and guided him, with an impatient hand. She had heard him work away, pant, kiss her, move, as clumsy and unsteady as a little animal learning to walk. Very soon thereafter, she had heard him let out a moan as he came.

When she went back to her bedroom, Don Rigoberto had not yet completed his toilet. Doña Lucrecia's heart was a runaway drum, a blind gallop. She felt amazed at her boldness and—she found it hard to believe—eager to embrace her husband. Her love for him had grown. The figure of the child was also there in her memory, filling her heart with tenderness. Was it possible that she had made love with him and was now about to make love with his father? Yes, it was. She felt neither shame nor remorse. Nor did she consider herself a cynic. It was as though the world were docilely submitting to her. An incomprehensible feeling of pride came over her. "I had a better orgasm tonight than last night, better than ever before," she heard Don Rigoberto say, later on. "I have no way to thank you for the happiness you give me." "Nor have I, my love," Doña Lucrecia whispered, trembling.

From that night on, she was certain that the clandestine meetings with the boy, however obscure and complicated, however difficult to explain, enriched her marital relation, taking it by surprise and thus giving it a fresh start. But what kind of morality is this, Lucrecia? she asked herself in astonishment. How is it possible that you've changed this way, at your age, overnight? She couldn't understand it, and made no attempt to do so. She preferred to bow to this contradictory situation, in which her acts challenged and violated her principles as she pursued that intense, dangerous rapture that happiness had become for her. One morning, on opening her eyes, the phrase "I have won sovereignty" came to her. She felt fortunate and emancipated, but could not have said what it was that she had been freed from.

Perhaps I don't have the feeling I'm doing something bad because Fonchito doesn't have that feeling either, she thought, stroking the child's body with her fingertips. To him, it's a game, a mischievous prank. And that's all there is between us; nothing more. He's not my lover. How could he be, at his age? What was he, then? Her little cupid, she told herself. Her *spintria*. The child whom Renaissance painters added to boudoir scenes so that, by contrast to their aura of purity, the love bout depicted would be the more ardent. Thanks to you, Rigoberto and I love and delight each other all the more, she thought, kissing him ever so lightly on the neck.

"I could explain to you why that painting is a portrait of you—even though it makes me feel funny all over," the youngster murmured, his head still buried in the pillows. "Would you like me to explain it to you, stepmother?"

"Oh, yes, please do." Doña Lucrecia fervently examined the sinuous little veins showing here and there just under his skin, like blue rivulets. "How can a painting in which there are no discernible figures, only geometric forms and colors, be my portrait?"

The boy raised his head, with a roguish look on his face.

"Just think about it and you'll see. Remember what the painting looks like and what you look like. I can't believe you won't tumble to the answer right away. It's as easy as pie! Guess what it is and I'll give you a reward."

"Was it only this morning that you noticed that that painting was a portrait of me?" Doña Lucrecia asked, more and more intrigued.

"You're getting warmer and warmer," the boy urged her on. "If you keep on the way you're going, you're bound to catch on to the answer. Oh, shame on you, stepmother!"

He let out another peal of laughter and hid himself between the sheets again. A little bird had perched on the windowsill and had begun peeping. It was a strident, jubilant sound that speared the morning and seemed to be celebrating the world, life. You're right to be happy, Doña Lucrecia thought. It's a beautiful world, worth living in. Peep, little bird, peep.

"So then, it's your secret portrait," Alfonsito murmured, drawing out each word and leaving mysterious pauses, seeking to create a theatrical effect. "What nobody knows or sees about you. Only me. And, oh yes, my papa, of course. If you don't guess now, you never will, stepmother."

He stuck his tongue out at her and made a face as he observed her with that liquid blue gaze beneath whose innocent crystal-clear surface Doña Lucrecia sometimes seemed to divine something perverse, like those tentacled creatures that dwell in the depths of ocean paradises. Her cheeks burned. Was Fonchito really hinting at what she had just intuitively sensed? Or, rather, did the youngster understand the meaning of what he was hinting at? Only halfway, doubtless, in a vague, instinctive way, beyond his power of reason. Was childhood, then, that amalgam of vice and virtue, of sanctity and sin? She tried to remember whether she, like Fonchito, had been, at some time long before, at once pure and filthy, but it was a memory beyond all recall. She rested her cheek once more against the child's tawny back and envied him. Oh, if only a person could always act with that half-conscious animal awareness with which he caressed her and made love to her, judging neither her nor himself! I hope you're spared suffering when you grow up, sweetie, she silently wished him.

"I think I've guessed," she said, after a moment. "But I don't dare tell you the answer, because, as it happens it's something dirty, Alfonsito."

"Of course it is," the youngster agreed, abashed. His cheeks were flaming red again. "But even if it's dirty, it's the truth, stepmother. That's how you are, too; it's not my fault. But what does it matter, since nobody will ever find out. Isn't that so?" And, without transition, in one of those unexpected changes of tone and subject in which he appeared all of a sudden to ascend or descend many steps on the staircase of age, he added: "Isn't it getting past time to go to the airport to pick up my papa? He'll feel so bad if we're not there to meet him."

What was happening between them had not changed in the slightest—as far as she could see, at any rate—Alfonso's relationship to Don Rigoberto; it seemed to Doña Lucrecia that the boy loved his father just as much and even more perhaps than before, to judge from the proofs of affection he offered him. Nor did he appear to experience in his father's presence the least uneasiness or give the least sign of a troubled conscience. "Things can't be this simple, nor everything turn out this well," she said to herself. And yet, thus far, they were just that simple, and everything was turning out exactly right. How much longer would this fantasy of perfect harmony last? She told herself once more that if she went about things intelligently and cautiously, nothing would intervene to shatter the dream-come-true that life had turned out to be for her. She was certain, moreover, that if this complicated situation went on, Don Rigoberto would be the fortunate beneficiary of her happiness. But, as always when she thought about this, a presentiment cast its shadow over the utopia: things turn out this way only in novels and in the movies, woman. Be realistic: sooner or later, the whole thing will end badly. Reality is never as perfect as fiction, Lucrecia.

"No, we still have time enough, my love. It's more than two hours still before the plane from Piura is due in. Provided it's on schedule."

"Well then, I'm going to sleep for a while. I feel so lazy." The youngster yawned. Leaning to one side, he sought the heat of Doña Lucrecia's body and lay his head on her shoulder. A moment later, he purred in a muffled voice: "Do you think if I get highest honors over everyone at the end of the school year, my papa will buy me the motorcycle I asked him for?"

"Yes, he'll buy it for you," she answered, hugging him gently, cooing to him as to a newborn babe. "If he doesn't, don't worry. I'll buy it for you."

As Fonchito slept, breathing slowly—she could feel, like echoes in her body, his symmetrical heartbeats—Doña Lucrecia, immersed in a peaceful drowsiness, stayed still so as not to awaken him. Half dissolved in dreams, her mind wandered amid a parade of images, but every so often one of them swam into focus in her consciousness, surrounded by a suggestive halo: the painting in the living room. What the boy had told her worried her a little and filled her with a mysterious malaise, for in that childish fantasy were hints of unsuspected depths and a morbid acuteness of insight.

Later, after getting up and eating breakfast, while

Alfonsito took a shower, she went down to the living room and stood contemplating the Szyszlo for a long time. It was as if she had never seen it before, as if the painting, like a serpent or a butterfly, had changed appearance and nature. That little boy is something to be taken seriously, she thought, troubled. What other surprises might lie hidden in that little head of a Hellenic demigod? That night, after picking Don Rigoberto up at the airport and listening to his account of the trip, they opened the presents he had brought back for her and the boy (as he did on every trip), and told him how pleased they were with them: cream custard, whistles, and two finely woven straw hats from Catacaos. Then the three of them had dinner together, like a happy family.

The couple retired to their bedroom at an early hour. Don Rigoberto's ablutions were briefer than usual. On joining each other in bed once more, husband and wife embraced passionately, as after a prolonged separation (in reality, just three days and two nights). That was how it had always been, ever since they'd been married. But after the initial caracoles in the darkness, when, faithful to the nightly liturgy, Don Rigoberto expectantly murmured: "Aren't you going to ask me who I am?" he heard this time an answer that broke the tacit pact: "No. You ask me, instead." There was an astonished pause, like a freeze frame in a film. But a few seconds later Don Rigoberto, a respecter of ritual, caught on and inquired eagerly: "Who, then, are you, darling?" "The woman in the painting in the living room, the abstract painting," she replied. There was another pause, a little laugh, half annoyed and half disappointed, a long electric silence. "This is no time to . . ." he started to say in a threatening voice. "I'm not joking," Doña Lucrecia interrupted him, closing his mouth with her lips. "That's who I am and I don't know why you haven't realized it before." "Help me, my love," he said, perking up, coming to life again, moving. "Explain to me. I want to understand." She explained and he understood.

Much later, as, after talking and laughing together, they prepared to take their rest, exhausted and happy, Don Rigoberto kissed his wife's hand with deep emotion:

"How much you've changed, Lucrecia. Not only do I love you with all my heart and soul now. I also admire you. I'm certain I have a great deal to learn from you still."

"At forty, people learn lots of things," she said tersely, caressing him. "Sometimes, Rigoberto, now for instance, it seems to me that I'm being born again. And that I'll never die."

Was that what sovereignty was?

Twelve.
Labyrinth of Love

At first, you will not see me or hear me, but you must be patient and keep looking. With perseverance and without preconceptions, freely and with desire, look. With your imagination unleashed and your penis ready and willing—preferably erect— look. One enters there as the novice nun enters the cloister or the lover the cavern of his beloved: resolutely, without petty calculations, giving everything, demanding nothing, and in one's soul the certainty that it is forever. Only on that condition, very gradually, the surface of dark purples and violets will begin to move, to become iridescent, to take on meaning and reveal itself to be what it in truth is, a labyrinth of love.

The geometrical figure in the middle band, at the exact center of the painting, that flat silhouette of a three-legged pachyderm, is an altar, a tabernacle, or if your mind is allergic to religious symbolism, a stage set. An exciting ceremony, with delightful and cruel reverberations, has just taken place, and what you see are its vestiges and its consequences. I know this because I have been the fortunate victim; the inspiration, the actress as well. Those reddish patches on the feet of the diluvial form are my blood and your sperm flowing forth and coagulating. Yes, my treasure, what is lying on the ceremonial stone (or, if you prefer, the pre-Hispanic stage prop), that viscous creature with mauve wounds and delicate membranes, black hollows and glands that discharge gray pus, is myself. Understand me: myself, seen from inside and from below, when you calcine me and express me. Myself, erupting and overflowing beneath your attentive libertine gaze of a male who has officiated with competence and is now contemplating and philosophizing.

Because you are there too, dearest. Looking at me as though autopsying me, eyes that look in order to see and the alert mind of an alchemist who exhaustively studies the phosphorescent formulas of pleasure. The one on the left, standing erect in the compartment with the dark brown glints, the one with the Saracen crescents on his head, draped in a mantle of live quills transmuted into a totem, the one with the spurs and the bright red feathers, the one with his back to me who is observing me: who could it be but you? You have just sat up and turned yourself into a curious onlooker. An instant ago you

Fernando de Szyszlo, *Road to Mendieta 10* (1977),
acrylic on canvas, private collection

were blind and on your knees between my thighs, kindling my fires like a groveling, diligent servant. Now you are taking your pleasure watching me take mine and reflecting. Now you know me for what I am. Now you would like to dissolve me in a theory.

Are we without shame? We are whole and free, rather, and as earthly as we can possibly be. They have removed our epidermises and melted our bones, bared our viscera and our cartilage, exposed to the light everything that during Mass or during amorous rites we celebrated together, grew, sweated, and excreted. They have left us without secrets, my love. That woman is what I am, slave and master, your offering. Slit open like a turtledove by love's knife. I: cracked apart and pulsing. I: slow masturbation. I: flow of musk. I: labyrinth and sensation. I: magic ovary, semen, blood, and morning dew. That is my face for you, at the hour of the senses. I am that when, for you, I shed my everyday skin and my feast-day one. That may perhaps be my soul. Yours.

Time has been suspended, naturally. There we shall not grow old or die. Illuminated by a moon that our intoxication has tripled, we will take our pleasure in that half twilight that already is raping the night. The real moon is the one in the center, as deep black as a raven's wing; the ones that escort it, the color of cloudy wine, a fiction.

Altruistic sentiments, metaphysics and history, neutral reasoning, good intentions and charitable deeds, solidarity with the species, civic idealism, sympathy toward one's fellow have also been done away with; all humans who are not you and me have been blotted out. Everything that might have distracted us or impoverished us at the hour of supreme egoism that the hour of love is has disappeared. Here, as is true as well of the monster and the god, nothing restrains or inhibits us.

This triadic abode—three feet, three moons, three spaces, three little windows, and three dominant colors—is the homeland of pure instinct and of the imagination that serves it, just as your serpentine tongue and your sweet saliva have both served me and used me. We have lost name and surname, face and hair, our air of respectability and our civil rights. But we have gained the power of magic, mystery, and bodily enjoyment. We were a woman and a man and now we are ejaculation, orgasm, and a fixed idea. We have become sacred and obsessive.

Our knowledge of each other is total. You are I and you, and you and I am you. Something as perfect and simple as a soaring swallow or the law of gravitation. Vice-ridden perversity—to put it in words in which we do not believe, words we both hold in contempt—is represented by those three exhibitionistic spectators in the upper left-hand corner. They are our eyes, the contemplation that we so eagerly practice—as you are now doing—the essential stripping bare that each one demands of the other in the love feast, and that fusion which can express itself adequately only by traumatizing syntax: I give your-self to me, you masturbate myself for you, let's you and me suck our selves.

Now leave off looking. Now close your eyes. Now, without opening them, look at me and look at your-self the way we were shown in that picture that so many look at and so few see. You now know that, even before we knew each other, loved each other, and married, someone, brush in hand, anticipated what horrendous glory we would be changed into by the happiness we learned to invent, each and every day and night of the morrow.

Thirteen.
Bad Words

"Isn't stepmother here?" Fonchito asked, dis-appointed.

"She'll be back shortly," Don Rigoberto an-swered, hurriedly clapping shut Sir Kenneth Clark's *The Nude*, lying open on his lap. With a brusque start of surprise, he returned to Lima, to his house, to his study, from the damp female vapors of Ingres's crowded *Turkish Bath*, in which he had been im-mersed. "She's gone off to play bridge with her lady friends. Come in, come in, Fonchito. Let's talk for a while."

The boy accepted the invitation with a nod of his head, his face wreathed in smiles. He came into the room and sat down on the edge of the big olive-colored leather easy chair, beneath the twenty-three hardbound volumes of the "Maîtres de l'amour" series, edited, with a preface, by Guillaume Apollinaire.

"Tell me how things are going at Santa María," his father encouraged him, as, hiding the book from sight behind his back, he crossed the room to replace it in the locked case where he kept his erotic treasures. "Are you keeping up with your studies all right? Are you having any trouble with English?"

He was doing very well and the teachers were very nice, Papa. He understood everything and had long conversations in English with Father Mackey; he was sure he'd be first in his class this year. He might even win the school prize for excellence.

Don Rigoberto beamed with satisfaction. Really, the boy brought him nothing but happiness. A model son; a good student, obedient, affectionate. He'd been lucky with him.

"Would you like a Coca-Cola?" he asked him. He had just poured himself two fingers of whiskey and was getting out ice. He handed Alfonso his glass and sat down beside him. "I must tell you something, son. I am very pleased with you and you can count on getting the motorcycle you asked me for. It'll be yours next week."

The youngster's eyes lighted up. He broke into a radiant smile.

"Thanks, Papa dear!" He put his arms around him and kissed him on the cheek. "The motorcycle I wanted so badly! That's super, Papa!"

Don Rigoberto disentangled himself, laughing.

He smoothed the boy's touseled hair, in a discreetly affectionate gesture.

"You have Lucrecia to thank for it," he added. "She insisted that I buy you your motorcycle right away, without waiting till exams were over."

"I knew it!" the boy exclaimed. "She's so good to me. Even better, I think, than my mama was."

"Your stepmother loves you a whole lot, my boy."

"And I love her lots," the youngster declared immediately, in fervent tones. "Why wouldn't I love her if she's the best stepmother in the world!"

Don Rigoberto took a sip of his whiskey and savored the taste of it: an agreeable fire ran down his tongue, his throat, and was now descending to his ribs. "Most pleasant lava," he extemporized. Who had this pretty son of his inherited his looks from? His face seemed to be surrounded by a radiant halo and was brimming over with freshness and wholesomeness. Not from him, surely. Nor from his mother, since Eloísa, though attractive and charming, had never had features as delicate as that, or such bright eyes and such transparent skin, or those curly locks of purest gold. A cherub, an adorable child, an archangel in a First Communion holy picture. It would be better for him if some little thing marred his perfect good looks just a bit when he grew up: women don't like doll-faced men.

"You don't know how happy it makes me that you get along so well with Lucrecia," he added after a moment. "I can tell you now that it was something that scared me a whole lot when we got married. That the two of you wouldn't be congenial, that you wouldn't accept her. That would have been most unfortunate for the three of us. Lucrecia, too, was very much afraid. Now, when I see how well you get along together, those fears make me laugh. In fact, the two of you love each other so much that, every so often, I'm downright jealous, since it seems to me that your stepmother loves you more than she does me and that you, too, are fonder of her than you are of your father."

Alfonso burst out laughing, clapping his hands, and Don Rigoberto imitated him, amused at his son's explosion of high spirits. A cat meowed somewhere in the distance. A car went past on the street with the radio turned up full blast, and for a few seconds they heard the trumpets and maracas of a song with a tropical beat. Then came the voice of Justiniana, humming in the pantry as she did a load of laundry in the washer.

"What does orgasm mean, Papa?" the boy suddenly asked.

Don Rigoberto was overtaken by a fit of coughing. He cleared his throat as he reflected: What should he answer? He did his best to assume a natural expression and managed not to smile.

"Well, it's not a bad word," he explained warily. "Certainly not. It has to do with sex life, with sensual enjoyment. It might be said, perhaps, that it is the peak of physical pleasure. Something that not only humans experience but many species of animals as well. They'll tell you about it in biology class, I'm sure. But, above all, don't get the idea that it's a dirty word. Where did you happen to come across it, my boy?"

"I heard my stepmother say it," Fonchito said. With an impish look, he raised a finger to his lips, enjoining him to secrecy. "I pretended I knew what it was. Don't let on to her that you explained to me what it was, Papa."

"No, I won't tell her," Don Rigoberto murmured. He took another sip of whiskey and, intrigued, looked closely at Alfonso. What was hiding there in that rosy-faced little head, behind that unfurrowed brow? Heaven only knew. Didn't they say that the soul of a child was a bottomless well? He thought: I mustn't ask one question more. He thought: I must change the subject. But morbid curiosity or the instinctive attraction of danger got the better of him, and, pretending indifference, he asked: "You heard that word you mentioned from your stepmother? Are you sure?"

The child nodded several times, with the same gay or roguish expression, or both at once. His cheeks were flushed and mischief twinkled in his eyes.

"She told me she had had a really splendid orgasm," he explained, in the eternally melodious voice of a nightingale. This time, Don Rigoberto's whiskey slipped out of his hands; numb with surprise, he saw the glass roll onto the lead-colored figures in the carpet of his study. The boy immediately bent down to pick it up. He handed it back to him, murmuring: "A good thing it was almost empty. Can I get you another, Papa? I know just how you like it—I've seen how my stepmother does it."

Don Rigoberto shook his head. Had he heard rightly? Yes, of course: that was what his big ears were for. To hear things properly. His brain had begun to crackle like a bonfire. This conversation had gone too far and it must be cut off once and for all, if something imponderable and extremely grave were not to occur. For an instant, he had the vision of a beautiful house of cards collapsing. His mind was totally clear as to what he ought to do. Enough of this: let's talk of something else. But this time, too, the siren song of the depths was more powerful than his reason and his good sense.

"What figment of your imagination is this, Foncho?" He spoke very slowly, but even so, his voice trembled. "How can you have heard your stepmother say such a thing? That can't be, my son."

The boy protested, vexed, with one hand upraised. "Oh, yes, it can, Papa. I certainly did hear her say it. And what's more, I was the one she said it to. Just yesterday afternoon. I give you my word. Why would I lie? Have I ever lied to you?"

"No, no, you're right. You always tell the truth."

He was unable to control the malaise that had

come over him like a fever. The uneasiness was a bumbling blowfly that kept bumping into his face, his arms, and he could neither swat it dead nor chase it away. He got to his feet and, walking slowly, went to fix himself another drink, something quite unlike him, since he never had more than one whiskey before dinner. When he returned to his chair, his eyes met Fonchito's blue-green ones: they were following his evolutions about the study with their usual gentle gaze. They smiled at him, and making an effort, he returned the smile.

"Ahem, ahem," Don Rigoberto cleared his throat, after a few seconds of ominous silence. He did not know what to say. Could it be possible that Lucrecia had shared confidences of that sort with him, that she had talked to the child about what they did at night? Of course not, what nonsense. They were products of Fonchito's imagination, something quite typical of his age: he was discovering wickedness, his sexual curiosity was surfacing, his awakening libido was prompting him to fantasize so as to bring conversations around to the fascinating taboo. Best to forget all that and dissolve the bad moment in trivial concerns.

"Don't you have homework for tomorrow?" he asked.

"I've already done it," the boy answered. "I had only one assignment, Papa. Free composition."

"Ah, I see. And what subject did you choose to write about?" Don Rigoberto persisted.

The boy's face flushed once again with innocent joy and Don Rigoberto suddenly felt a deerlike fear. What was happening? What was going to happen?

"Well, about her, Papa, about who she was going to turn out to be," Fonchito said, clapping his hands. "I called it 'In Praise of the Stepmother.' What do you think of that for a title?"

"Very good. Just fine," Don Rigoberto replied. And almost without thinking, with a hearty laugh that rang false, he added: "It sounds like the title of a little erotic novel."

"What does erotic mean?" the child asked gravely.

"Having to do with physical love," Don Rigoberto enlightened him. He was taking one sip of his drink after another, without noticing. "Certain words such as that take on their full meaning only with the passage of time, thanks to experience, something far more important than definitions. All that will come about little by little; there is no reason for you to be in a hurry, Fonchito."

"Whatever you say, Papa," the child agreed, blinking: his lashes were enormous and cast an iridescent violet-tinged shadow on his pupils.

"Do you know what? I'd like to read that 'Praise of the Stepmother.' May I?"

"Of course, Papa dear," the child said enthusiastically. He leapt to his feet and went off at a run. "That way, if there's a mistake anywhere, you'll correct it for me."

In the few minutes that it took Fonchito to return, Don Rigoberto felt his malaise grow. Too much whiskey perhaps? No, what a thought. Did that pressure on his temples mean that he was becoming ill? At the office, there were several people down with the flu. No, that wasn't it. Well, then, what was it? He remembered the verse from *Faust* that had moved him so deeply when he was a boy: "I love him who desires the impossible." He would have liked that to be his motto in life, and, in a certain way, though secretly, he harbored the feeling that he had attained that ideal. Why, then, did he now have the distressing premonition that an abyss was opening at his feet? What sort of danger threatened? How? Where? He thought: It is absolutely impossible that Fonchito could have heard Lucrecia say: "I had a splendid orgasm." An irresistible fit of laughter came over him and he laughed, though joylessly, with a painful grin that the glass of the bookcase full of erotica beamed back at him. There Alfonso was, with a notebook in his hand. He handed it to his father without a word, looking him straight in the eye, with that pure-blue gaze of his, so calm and candid that, as Lucrecia said, "it made people feel dirty."

Don Rigoberto put on his glasses and turned on the floor lamp. He began to read aloud the clear letters so carefully traced in black ink, but in the middle of the first sentence he fell silent. He went on reading to himself, moving his lips slightly and blinking frequently. Soon his lips stopped moving. They slowly gaped open, sagging at the corners, giving his entire face a dull, stupid expression. A little thread of saliva drooped from between his teeth and stained the lapels of his suit coat, though he did not appear to notice, since he did not wipe it away. His eyes moved from left to right, now rapidly, now slowly, and at times they went back from right to left, as if they had not understood correctly or as if they were unable to accept that what they had read was really written there on the page. Not once, as the slow, endless reading proceeded, did Don Rigoberto's eyes leave the notebook to look at the child, who, doubtless, was still there in the same place, keeping a close watch on his reactions, waiting for him to finish reading and say and do what he ought to say and do. What ought he to say? What ought he to do? Don Rigoberto could feel that his hands were soaking wet. A few drops of sweat slid down his forehead onto the notebook and made the ink spread in formless blots. Swallowing hard, he managed to come up with the thought: Loving the impossible has a price that must be paid sooner or later.

He made a supreme effort, closed the notebook, and looked up. Yes, there Fonchito was, watching him with his beautiful, beatific face. That's what Lucifer must have looked like, he thought as he raised the empty glass to his mouth to take a swallow. From the tinkle of the crystal against his teeth he realized how badly his hand was trembling.

"What does this mean, Alfonso?" he blurted. His back teeth, his tongue, his jaw hurt. He did not recognize his own voice.

"What, Papa?"

The boy looked at him as though he did not understand what had come over him.

"What's the meaning of these . . . fantasies?" he stammered, from amid the terrible confusion that was torturing his soul. "Have you gone mad, child? How could you have made up such filthy stories?"

He fell silent because he did not know what else to say and felt disgusted and completely taken aback by what he had said. The radiance of the child's face began to slowly fade as a sad expression came over it. He contemplated him, not understanding, with a vague look of pain in his eyes, and bewilderment as well, but not a shadow of fear.

Finally, after a few seconds, Don Rigoberto heard him say what, amid the horror that froze his heart, he was waiting for him to say. "What do you mean, stories I made up, Papa? When everything I tell about is true, when it all happened just the way I say."

At that moment, so perfectly synchronized that he imagined it to have been determined by fate or by the gods, Don Rigoberto heard the front door open and Lucrecia's melodious voice bid the butler good evening. He managed to come up with the thought that the splendid, original nocturnal world of dreams and desires given free rein that he had so carefully erected had just burst like a soap bubble. And, all of a sudden, his ruined fantasy desired, desperately, to be transmuted: he was a solitary being, chaste, freed of appetites, safe from all the demons of the flesh and sex. Yes, yes, that was how he was. The anchorite, the hermit, the monk, the angel, the archangel who blows the celestial trumpet and descends to the garden to bring the glad tidings to pure and pious maidens.

"Hello there, my big cavalier and my little one!" Doña Lucrecia sang out from the doorway of the study.

Her snow-white hand let loose flying kisses for father and son.

Fourteen.
The Rosy Youth

The midday heat made me drowsy and I did not
sense his arrival. But I opened my eyes and there
he was, at my feet, in a rose-colored light. Was he
really there? Yes, I did not dream him. He must
have come in through the back door, which my parents had left open, or perhaps leapt over the garden
wall, one that any lad can easily jump over.

Who was he? I don't know, but he was there, I'm
certain, in this very corridor, kneeling at my feet. I
saw him and heard him. He has just left. Or, should
I say, vanished in thin air? Yes: kneeling at my feet.
I don't know why he knelt, but he didn't do it to
mock me. From the beginning he treated me so
gently and so reverently and gave proof of such respect and humbleness toward me that the anxiety
that overtook me on seeing an outsider so close at
hand evaporated like dew in sunlight. How is it pos-

sible that I felt no apprehension on finding myself alone with a stranger? With someone who, moreover, entered the garden of my house I know not how. I don't understand it. But all the time that the young man was here, speaking to me as one speaks to an important woman, not the modest young girl that I am, I felt more safeguarded than when my parents are at my side, or when I am in the Temple, on the Sabbath.

How handsome he was! I ought not to use the word, but in all truth I had never seen such a harmonious and gentle being, so seemly, with such a subtle voice. I could scarcely look at him; each time my eyes alighted on his delicate cheeks, his candid brow, or the long lashes of his great eyes full of goodness and wisdom, I felt a warm dawn on my face. Can this be, if magnified throughout the body, what young girls feel when they fall in love? That warmth that does not come from outside but from within the body, from the depths of the heart? My girlfriends in the village often talk of this, I know, but when I draw near they fall silent, for they know that I am very shy and that certain subjects—this one, love, for instance—embarrass me so much that my face turns scarlet and I begin to stammer. Is it wrong to be that way? Esther says that, seeing how timid and bashful I am, I will never know what love is. And Deborah keeps trying to encourage me: "You have to be bolder, or your life will be a sad one."

But the rosy youth said that I am the chosen one,

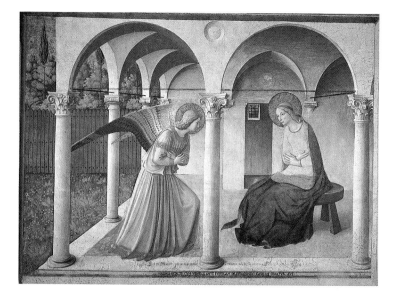

Fra Angelico, *The Annunciation* (*c.* 1437),
fresco, Monastery of San Marco, Florence

that, among all women, they have singled me out. Who? What for? Why? What good or bad thing have I done for someone to favor me? I know very well how unnoteworthy I am. In the village there are girls much more comely and hardworking, stronger, more intelligent, more courageous. Why would I be chosen, then? Because I get along well with everyone? Because of the affection with which I milk our little goat and the happiness I find in doing simple everyday tasks, such as cleaning the house, watering the garden, and preparing my parents' food? I do not believe I have any other merits than those, if that is what they are, and not defects. Deborah once said to me: "You have no aspirations, Mary." Perhaps that is true. What can I do if that is the way I was born: I like life and the world seems beautiful to me just as it is. Perhaps that's why they say I'm simple. Doubtless I am, since I have always avoided complications. But I do have certain ardent desires. I'd like it if my little nanny goat never died, for example. When she licks my hand, the thought comes to me that she will die one day, and pain grips my heart. It is not good to suffer. I would also like it if no one suffered.

The young man said absurd things, but in such a melodious and sincere way that I didn't dare laugh. That they would bless me and bless the fruit of my womb. That is what he said. Might he be a magician? Could he have been using those words as an incantation for or against something or someone? I couldn't think how to ask him such a question. At those words of his, all I could do was stammer what I answer when my elders teach me a lesson or reprimand me: "Very well, I shall do as I ought, sire." And I covered my belly with my hands in fright. Can "fruit of my womb" mean that I will have a child? How happy that would make me. I'd like it to be a son as sweet and mysterious as the young man who came to see me.

I don't know whether I should be happy or sad because of that visit. I have a presentiment that, after it, my life will change. In what way? Will it be to my good fortune or to my misfortune? Why, amid the joy I feel when I remember the sweet words of that young man, do I suddenly feel afraid, as if the earth were suddenly about to open and I were to see at my feet an abyss bristling with fearful monsters trying to force me to leap?

He said very nice things, which sounded most pleasing, but difficult to understand. "Extraordinary destiny, supernatural destiny," among others. What was he referring to? My nature, to the contrary, predisposes me to the ordinary, the everyday. Everything that draws attention or is out of place, any gesture or act that violates tradition or custom, stops me short and disconcerts me. When someone goes too far and makes a fool of himself in my presence, my face flames and I feel for him. I am comfortable only when others do not note my presence. "Mary is so unobtrusive she seems invisible," Rachel, the girl next door, teases me. I like it when she says that. It's true: to me, to pass unnoticed is to be happy.

But that does not mean that I have no dreams and lack feelings. It's just that I have never felt attracted by the extraordinary. My girlfriends leave me open-mouthed with astonishment when I hear them: they would like to travel, to have many servants, to marry a king. Such fantasies frighten me. What would I do in other lands, among people different from mine, hearing other languages? And what a lamentable queen I would make, since I lose my voice and my hands tremble when someone I do not know is listening to me. What I ask of life is an upright husband, healthy children, and a peaceful existence, without hunger and without fear. What did that young man mean by "extraordinary, supernatural destiny"? My shyness kept me from answering him as I should have: "I am not prepared for that, I'm not the one you are speaking of. Go visit beautiful Deborah instead, or Judith, who is so determined, or go to the house of Rachel, the intelligent one. How can you announce to me that I shall be queen of men? How can you say that they will pray to me in all tongues and that my name will traverse the centuries as stars wheel across the sky? You have the wrong girl and the wrong house, sire. I am far too humble to be so exalted. I almost don't exist."

Before leaving, the youth leaned down and kissed

the hem of my tunic. For a second I saw his back: it had a rainbow on it, as though the wings of a butterfly had alighted there.

He is gone now and has left my head full of doubts. Why did he address me as señora if I am still an unmarried girl? Why did he call me queen? Why did I discover a gleam of tears in his eyes when he prophesied that I would suffer? Why did he call me mother if I am a virgin? What is happening? What is going to become of me after this visit?

Epilogue

"Don't you ever feel remorse, Fonchito?" Justiniana suddenly asked. She was picking up, folding, and placing on a chair the clothes that the youngster was offhandedly taking off and then tossing her way with basketball passes. His crystalline voice was astonished. "For what, Justita?"

Leaning over to pick up a pair of argyles with garnet-red and green diamonds, she spied him in the mirror over the bureau: Alfonso had just sat down on the edge of the bed and was putting on his pajama pants, first bending his legs, then stretching them out. Justiniana saw his slender white feet with pink heels peek out the bottom of the pants legs and his ten toes wriggle as though doing exercises. Finally her eyes met his, and he beamed her a smile.

"Don't look at me that way, as though butter wouldn't melt in your mouth, Foncho," she said, straightening up. She rubbed the small of her back and sighed, looking at the boy in puzzlement. She sensed that, once again, anger was about to get the better of her. "I'm not her. You can't buy me, or fool me with that angelic smile of yours. Tell me the truth, for once. Don't you feel the least remorse? Not even one little twinge?"

Alfonso hooted with laughter, flinging his arms wide open, and let himself fall backward onto the bed. He kicked his legs in the air, passing and receiving an imaginary basketball. It was a hearty, eloquent laugh, without a trace of mockery or malice as far as Justiniana could tell. Lord, she thought, who can possibly understand this cheeky little brat?

"I swear to God I don't know what you're talking about," the child exclaimed, sitting upright and sealing the oath by kissing his crossed fingers with conviction. "Or are you asking me a riddle, Justita?"

"Get in bed, so you don't catch cold. I don't feel at all like taking care of you."

Alfonso immediately obeyed her. He leapt up, raised the bedcovers, slid nimbly between the sheets, and settled the pillow behind his back. Then he sat there, gazing up at the girl with a pampered, spoiled look in his eyes, as though about to receive a reward. His hair fell over his forehead and his big blue eyes gleamed in the semidarkness in which they found themselves, for the light from the little bedside lamp extended no farther than his cheeks. His lipless mouth was half open, revealing a row of gleaming white teeth he had just finished brushing.

"I'm talking about Doña Lucrecia, you little devil, as you know very well, so don't play dumb," she said. "Aren't you sorry for what you did to her?"

"Oh, her," the child exclaimed, disappointed, as though the subject were too obvious and too boring to be of interest to him. He shrugged and added without the slightest hesitation: "Why should I be sorry? If she'd been my mama, I might have been. But was she?"

There was no animosity or anger, either in his tone of voice or in his face; but the indifference was the very thing that irked Justiniana.

"You fixed things so that your papa would throw her out of this house like a dog," she murmured in a dull, sad voice, with her head turned the other way, her eyes staring at the gleaming parquet floor. "You lied, first to her and then to him. You fixed things so they'd separate, when they were so happy. She must be the most wretched woman in the world now, on account of you. And Don Rigoberto, too. Since he separated from your stepmother, he's like a lost soul. Can't you see how much he's aged in just a few days? Doesn't that give you the least remorse, either? And he's turned into a pious hypocrite and a prude, the like of which I've never seen. That's what happens when people sense that they're at death's door. And all because of you, you devil!"

She turned toward the boy in sudden fright, thinking that she had said more than was prudent. After what had happened, she didn't trust anything or anybody in this house. Fonchito's head had moved toward her, the golden cone of lamplight surrounding it like a crown. He seemed dumbfounded.

"But I didn't do anything, Justita," he stammered, his eyes blinking, and she could see his Adam's apple wobbling in his throat like an edgy little animal. "I never lied to anybody, least of all to my papa."

Justiniana felt her face burning.

"You lied to everybody, Foncho!" she said in a loud, clear voice. But she fell silent immediately, clapping her hand over her mouth, for at that moment the sound of water running in the washbasin upstairs reached her ears. Don Rigoberto had begun his nightly ablutions, which, since Doña Lucrecia's departure, were much less prolonged. He went to bed at an early hour every night now and could no longer be heard humming songs from operettas as he made his toilet. When Justiniana spoke again, she did so in a low voice, reprimanding the boy with her index finger: "And you lied to me, too, naturally. To think that I swallowed that story that you were going to kill yourself because Doña Lucrecia didn't love you."

And now, for the first time, the boy's face suddenly showed signs of indignation.

"It wasn't a lie," he said, seizing her arm and

shaking her. "It was true, or as good as true. If my stepmother went on treating me the way she did back then, I would have killed myself. I swear I would have, Justita!"

The girl jerked her arm away and left the bedside. "Don't swear in vain, or God may punish you," she murmured.

She went over to the window, and as she parted the curtains, she noticed that stars were shining here and there in the sky. She stood there looking at them in surprise. How odd to see those little twinkling lights instead of the usual dull fog. When she turned around, the boy had picked up a book from the night table and, adjusting the pillow to fit comfortably behind his back, was settling down to read. He gave every appearance of being, once again, calm and contented, at peace with his conscience and the world.

"Just tell me one thing, Fonchito."

Upstairs, the water was running in the washbasin with an even, steady murmur, and on the roof two cats wailed, fighting or fornicating.

"What, Justita?"

"Did you plan the whole thing from the beginning? That pantomime of loving her so much, that business of climbing up on the roof to spy on her as she bathed, the letter threatening to kill yourself. Was it all just a big story you made up? Just so she'd love you and then, after that, you'd be able to go to your papa and claim she was corrupting you?"

The boy put the book back down on the night table, marking his place with a pencil. His face was disarmed by a hurt look.

"I never said she was corrupting me, Justita!" he exclaimed, shocked, flailing the air with one of his hands. "You're making that up. Don't try to trick me. My papa was the one who said she was corrupting me. All I did was write that composition, telling about what we did. The truth, that is. None of it was a lie. It's not my fault he threw her out. Maybe what he said was true. She might have been corrupting me. If my papa said that, it must be so. Why are you so concerned about it? Would you rather have gone off with her than stay here in this house?"

Justiniana leaned back against the bookshelf where Alfonso kept his tales of adventure, his school pennants and diplomas and class photos. She half closed her eyes and thought: I should have left some time ago, it's true.

Since Doña Lucrecia's departure, she had had a foreboding that some sort of danger lay in wait for her here, and was on edge all the time, with the constant feeling that if she let down her guard even for a moment, she, too, would fall into a trap and come out of it in worse shape than the stepmother. It had been imprudent of her to confront the boy that way. She would never do so again, because even if Fonchito was still a child as far as age went, he really wasn't one, but instead someone more perverse and devious than all the grown men she knew. Yet, even so, looking at that sweet little face, those doll's features, who would ever have thought it.

"Are you mad at me about something?" she heard him say contritely.

"No, I'm not," she answered, heading toward the door. "Don't read very long. You've school tomorrow. Good night."

"Justita."

She turned to look at him, one hand already on the doorknob.

"What?"

"Please don't be mad at me." He looked at her with pleading eyes, batting his long eyelashes; he beseeched her with his mouth puckered in a half pout and the dimples in his cheeks pulsing. "I love you lots. But you hate me. Isn't that so, Justita?"

His voice sounded as though he were about to burst into tears.

"I don't hate you, silly. Why would I?"

Upstairs, the water continued to run, with a uniform sound, interrupted by brief spasms, and from time to time Don Rigoberto's footsteps could be heard as well, going from one side of the bathroom to the other.

"If you really don't hate me, give me just one good-night kiss. Like before, I mean. Have you forgotten?"

She hesitated for a moment, but then acquiesced. She went over to the bed, bent down, and gave him a quick kiss on the top of his head. But the boy kept a tight hold on her, flinging his arms about her neck, and fooling around and cutting up, till Justiniana smiled at him despite herself. When he acted that way, sticking out his tongue, rolling his eyes, moving his head to and fro, raising and lowering his shoulders, she didn't see him as the cruel, cold devil he had inside him, but as the pretty little boy he was on the outside.

"Enough of that. Stop your clowning and go to sleep now, Foncho."

She kissed the top of his head again and sighed. And though she had promised herself that she would not say another word on the subject, she heard herself blurt out, contemplating those golden locks grazing her nose: "Did you do all that on account of Doña Eloísa? Because you didn't want anyone to replace your mama? Because you couldn't bear to have Doña Lucrecia take her place in this house?"

She could feel the boy tense up, but he said nothing, as though thinking hard what his answer should be. Then the little arms entwined about her neck pressed her to lower her head so that the tiny lipless mouth might draw closer to her ear. But instead of hearing him whisper the secret that she expected, she felt him nibble and kiss her on the top of her ear and just behind, till she tingled all over.

"I did it for you, Justita," she heard him murmur, with velvety tenderness, "not for my mama. So she'd leave this house and leave the three of us alone together: my papa, you, and I. Because you're the one I . . ."

The girl suddenly felt the child's mouth come down hard on hers.

"Good lord, good lord." She freed herself from his arms, pushing him, shaking him. She staggered out of the room, rubbing her mouth, crossing herself. It seemed to her that unless she got a breath of fresh air her heart would burst with rage. "My god, my god."

Outside now, in the hallway, she heard Fonchito laugh once more. Not sarcastically, not making mock of her flushed cheeks and brimming indignation. With genuine delight, as though enjoying a splendid joke. Fresh, round and full, healthy, childish, his laughter drowned out the sound of the water in the washbasin, appeared to fill the whole night and mount to those stars which, for once, had appeared in the muddy sky of Lima.